BEA FRANZ

I0575473

EXIT HERE

TRAPPED IN A WORLD OF HATE AND TERROR

Thriller

EXIT HERE Copyright©2001
by Buddhismus Stiftung Diamantweg der Karma Kagyü Linie.
Issued under the seal of the United States Copyright Office,
the Library of Congress.

Published by TUBUK digital
TUBUK digital is an imprint of Open Publishing Rights GmbH
Cover design: Rafal Olech

ISBN: 978-3-95595-058-3

Visit our homepage:
www.tubuk-digital.de

For my Buddhist Teacher,
for my Lama, for my Friend,
for Lama Ole Nydahl

Acknowledgements

My deepest and heartfelt thanks to all friends on the way
who helped to make the realisation of Exit Here possible:

Anthony Hopson, Alexander Press, Astrid Ferrara Santamaria,
Berno Kuerten, Christa Albrecht, Dmitry Kudinov, Emanuela
Agostino, Eva Sencic, Irma Cantoni, Kai Burmeister, Marco
Calipari, Mikel Klein, Milena Rimassa, Norbert Wolf, Patricia
Press-Schaffrick, Peter Arras, Peter Fasshauer, Renate Schwarz,
Rafal Olech, Sigrid Frank, Stephen James, Tanja Boehnke, Thilo
Schreiber, Vagid Ragimow, Vanni Ferrara Santamaria, Wojtek
Tracewski, Tomek Lehnert, Victor Shmarkovsky & Jakob Sintschnig.

Death is not
a problem.
The problem is
a life without
meaning.

Lama Ole Nydahl

AUTHOR'S NOTE

EXIT HERE was born as an original idea for a feature film
based upon Buddhist teachings about Death, Intermediary
State and Rebirth as taught by Lama Ole Nydahl.

EXIT HERE is about freedom and the courage of those who protect
it. The aim of the film is to show the audience how to deal with the
fear of terrorist attacks, in particular, with the fear of death. Due to
9/11, the movie industry either didn't want to touch Exit Here or
just wasn't interested in a meaningful, gripping and deeply touching
story or it could be that the time wasn't ripe for it yet. For more than
15 years the feature film project exit here lay idle to resurface like a
phoenix from its ashes.
Now it is available for everyone, everywhere as a thriller
and fiction in a printed and an e-book form!

CONTENTS

Part I

A Sticky Affair

A Sticky Affair

1. Hostage Taking.

In the summer of 2001, Elista the capital city of the Republic of Kalmykia, Russia, is still characterized by the decay of Soviet-built institutions.

Old-fashioned clothing and buildings unveil life in the south of Russia. Children are playing and laughing in the street in front of the big iron door of a dilapidated three-story school. A nine-year old boy called Ivan pulls at the pigtail of a blond girl named Sveta. She starts crying. The boy approaches her apologetically and hands her some American chewing gum. She stops crying and accepts it with a smile.

A bell rings and a friendly woman, the headmistress, opens the iron door. The schoolchildren run into the building heading for the second floor.

Eight men with dark-bearded faces wrap camouflage scarves around their heads to conceal their identity. They sit in the back of a truck and load their Kalashnikovs. The truck passes the Buddhist Stupa in Elista. One of the dark bearded faces points his gun at the Stupa and hisses:

"Idols. I'll blow it up."

The one beside him raises his Kalashnikov:

"Later. God is great."

The headmistress still stands by the door. A young woman crosses the street and approaches her. They shake hands. The headmistress smiles at the young woman:

"Let's meet with the children and the other teachers. They're waiting for us in the main hall upstairs."

The young woman hesitates. The headmistress takes the young woman's hand:

"Don't worry. The children are great. You'll get along fine with them."

The street in front of the school is silent and empty now, the iron door creaks in the wind. The muzzle of a Kalashnikov appears around the edge of the door followed by seven dark-bearded faces wrapped in camouflage scarves.

2. Strawberry Fields Forever.

Russian rock music blasts from the radio of a modest apartment of the Plattenbauten – a large-panel system building in the outskirts of St. Petersburg, the second largest city in Russia.

It is 6:00 in the morning. There are cigarette butts overflowing from an ashtray on the table in the simple living room as well as several empty vodka bottles, half eaten watermelons in the garbage-can in the kitchen, evidence of a wild birthday party the night before.

Two young athletically built men, Sergey and Andrey, are arm wrestling. Sasha and Dmitry, the same type of men turn their heads as an older man named Yuri steps into the room smoking a cigarette and smiling.

Yuri is a medium-sized man, has dark hair and alert bright blue eyes. He wears a tight black t-shirt with an American slogan and black jeans. The t-shirt shows his muscular chest and strong arms. Sergey wins the arm wrestling match. Andrey is a bit embarrassed and jokingly looks up at Yuri:

"Commander, it's unbelievable, your training methods have really helped. This child has become bloody strong."

Yuri grins broadly: "Or you just had a glass too many."

The others laugh. Kirill rubs a deep scar on his neck while Mikhail puts out his cigarette and grabs a guitar. Mikhail asks looking at Sergey:

"What shall I play for you then?"

Sergey, happy to celebrate his birthday with all his friends and his commander answers:

"What about Strawberry fields forever?"

Mikhail agrees pensively:

"Hmmm, an old Beatles' song. Why not?"

Mikhail starts playing the song.

3. A World of Terror.

The sun sets over London, the capital city of England and the most populated city in the United Kingdom with a metropolitan area of over 13 million inhabitants.

The sun setting creates a range of the most beautiful shades of red and the big windows of the stately home at Oxford street appear to be golden.

The entrance of the building is decorated with a brass sign engraved with FireWorks International. Inside of the building on the first floor a young editor of the private television broadcasting FireWorks International is looking at the footage of The Rich & Famous together with a young woman.

It's the celebration of an international music award in Los Angeles. White limousines drive up in front of the celebration building. The doors of a limousine open. A woman gets out. She is wearing a transparent dress.

A finger, adorned with a beautiful ring belonging to Alba Smith, an Italian-American woman in her late twenties points at the monitor. Her intense green eyes have the same intense green colour as the precious emerald of her ring. She addresses the young editor:

"Vincent, look at her! Do you know how old she is?"

Vincent amusedly answers:

"She looks like she's 30. But she can't be. I know that she's been in the business for some time already."

Alba makes a comment about the star:

"I think she looks better than ever. At least on the screen. She's 55 actually."

Vincent freezes the picture, although Alba continues with her comment:

"She's living proof that expensive plastic surgery and a lot of hard work in the gym help you look young. Doesn't she look ageless?"

Vincent pretends to be indignant:

"You may call it ageless! I think she looks like a caricature of herself when she was 30."

A noise in the back makes Alba turn around.

In the doorway stands Cynthia Broccoli, the head of FireWorks International. She is in her late forties and wearing a provocative party dress. Cynthia edges herself into the conversation saying:

"Ageless? She spends a fortune to look like that."

Alba who did not expect to see her boss in the TV studio looks at Cynthia puzzled: "What are you doing here? Is the party over?"

Cynthia answers that the party was quite boring and complains that her dress was not appreciated.

Alba reassures Cynthia that her new look is gorgeous and asks: "It's Vandani. Isn't it? It must have cost a fortune."

Cynthia smiles, looks down at her dress and nods: "Well, Richard bought it for me. He likes me wearing clothes like these". Cynthia turns around to the frozen picture on the screen saying: "We are more or less the same age. Maybe I should start to have plastic surgery as well".

Cynthia looks at Alba puzzled. Alba does not react. Cynthia changes the subject:

"Anyway, I am not here for that. Steven had a car-accident. He's in hospital." Alba is concerned:

"Anything serious?" "No, fortunately not. A few bruises and a mild concussion. It means he can't fly in case there has been any damage to the blood vessels in his brain."

Alba looks at Cynthia slightly irritatedly and asks:

"Fly where?"

"To Edinburgh. Steven was due to go to an international anti-terrorism experts meeting. Only a few journalists have been invited to participate."

Alba nervously replies: "I still have to finish The Rich & Famous. I need to do the interviews with Harry Rocky and Count Carrano. I'm flying to New York tomorrow to see them."

Cynthia sternly says to Alba: "You'd better cancel your flight until after the meeting in Edinburgh."

Alba sighs and says: "Cynthia, you know how difficult it was to get time to interview those people."

"Yes, I know. Well, Major Jefferson is Steven's contact. He's the leader of the American delegation. He's agreed to provide you with the missing information which Steven needed for A World of Terror. I can't send anybody else now."

Alba insists: "You know that I'm not prepared for anything like this!"

Cynthia does not answer to Alba's objection and instead hands Alba an envelope:

"Here's a short briefing and your ticket."

Alba indignantly states:

"I have never had anything to do with the world of terror and besides, it's my mother's 60th birthday tomorrow. You know I don't see her so often because she lives in New York. Look!"

Alba takes a mobile phone from her handbag: "I was going to give her this present. It is her first mobile phone."

"I'm sorry Alba, but you know how things are sometimes."

In the background there is a loud bang. Alba jumps. Champagne bottles are being opened.

Cynthia turns around and walks out of the office.

Vincent apologises and freezes the footage tape once more.

4. Slippery Like A Snake.

Sergey's mother, who is about 50 years old, comes in with a huge plate of fried potatoes and fish. She puts it on the table and listens to the last bars of the song. Her face brightens up and smiles at Mikhail:

"How wonderful. I first heard this song when I was once in the West with Sergey's father. Nine months later Sergey was born".

Sasha is looking at Yuri trying to be serious: "Commander, that means you are going to have to be careful. Stay away from the blondes."

Sergey curiously asks:

"Commander, are you going abroad?"

Kirill grins at Sergey: "Your commander has been invited to Scotland to report to an international conference. He has to tell them how strong you've become!" Sergey seriously inquires: "Is that true?" Yuri answers with a twinkle in his eyes: "Actually, Kirill is right. I am going to talk to them about our Motherland's contribution to their security." Yuri clears his throat and rests his arms on the table:

"Ladies and gentlemen, instead of my speech on behalf of the Russian parliament and our president I have to inform you that we are in fact trapped in a very difficult situation. One very dangerous individual is amongst us. He's slippery like a snake, and we never know where he is. When he has trapped you, you have no chance to get out alive."

Sasha joins Yuri by saying: "That's it. It's all over. We may as well prepare to die." Sergey, still very earnest, addresses his commander: "But Captain, you have never been defeated! And none of your men have ever died. How can you talk like this?"

Yuri shakes his head and now talks about his genuine concern:

"Well, he really is one of the most difficult little toads to catch."

A guitar string breaks. Mikhail looks up. His eyes meet Dmitry's eyes. Dmitry expressionlessly remarks:

"Ali."

Yuri's eyes become ice-cold for an instant then he laughs:

"No, that's Sergey!"

The men turn to Sergey and slap him on the back laughing. Sergey is embarrassed but flattered at the same time. Yuri pacifies: "Luckily for us he has recently joined Spetsnaz. Those terrorists don't stand a chance. Okay, the conference is over. Let Sergey get to work." There's much applause from Yuri's men. Yuri grins, grabs Sergey by the shoulder, brings him to his feet and hugs him warmly. The men thank Sergey's mother for the food and start to eat. Yuri's pager beeps. He gets up, walks to the phone and dials a number:

"Hello, this is Captain Sokolov speaking. Yes, Sir. Immediately." Yuri hangs up and turns to his men:

"We're leaving."

Immediately the men stand up, grab their jackets and leave the apartment. With a deep sigh Sergey's mother looks at the breakfast on the table. Yuri embraces her saying:

"I'm sorry that we have to leave so soon. Sergey should be back this evening."

5. No one can escape death.

The headmistress and the young woman enter the big hall on the second floor. The children get up from their chairs and look at the new teacher with curiosity. The headmistress and the teacher walk to the stage where the other five teachers stand lined up behind a table. She motions to everyone to sit down. Smiling at the young female teacher then at the children and finally at her staff she says:

"Lena Parilova is our new teacher. She has come all the way down from the north, from Murmansk, to marry Dr. Batra. Would you like to know more about Murmansk in the north of Russia?"

The children nod. Pleased, the young teacher smiles:

"Okay, children. First I will draw you a map and show you where it is." She turns around toward the blackboard. A picture of a strange-looking beast with three blood-shot eyes and enormous fangs and holding a big wheel in his hairy paws stares down at her. Lena Parilova is surprised:

"What's that?"

Sveta stands up and responds seriously:

"That's Yama, the Tibetan Lord of Death."

The young female teacher looks at the headmistress. She nods. Encouraged, Sveta adds:

"He reminds us that all people and animals have to die. No one can escape death..."

The girl can't finish the sentence. She is interrupted by seven black masked men who burst through the door, shouting commands and pointing their Kalashnikovs. They force everybody to go to one corner of the hall.

Ivan, the little boy, breaks away from the others and runs to the open door. One of the black masked men, obviously the leader moves quickly and fires into the body of the boy. The others cry helplessly with horror as the dead body falls to the ground.

The masked man who has just killed Ivan shouts:

"Shut the fuck up! On your knees, I don't want to see the faces of pigs! Heads down! Turn to the wall!"

The headmistress tearfully tries to make the children understand that they must follow their orders.

The masked man who has just killed Ivan takes out his mobile phone and says with a malicious grin:

"Good morning Mr. President. Sorry for disturbing your important business but we have a difficult situation here. Maybe you can help."

6. Hostage Freeing.

Yuri and his men have arrived at Elista airport. Dressed in black combat overalls they jump out of the aircraft carrying their equipment in worn-out bags. Three officers escort the head of the local police as he approaches Yuri. They salute each other.

The head of the police informs Yuri: "Commander, the terrorists have changed their demands. Now they want six of their people to be released from prison in exactly 15 minutes. If we don't comply, they're going to shoot the first hostage, the second one 15 minutes later, then the third in three quarters of an hour."

Yuri sums up:

"250 hostages, 6 teachers, 8 terrorists. The hostages are all on the second floor?" The head of the police agrees:

"That is correct, Commander. Seven terrorists are in the building and one is on the roof. We've heard shots already."

Yuri inquires:

"Is there a three-story building nearby?"

"There's one in the back of the school."

The head of the police hands Yuri the floor plan of the school building and a map of the town.

Yuri asks: "Are the helicopter and ambulances ready?"

"Comrade Commander, everything is here and at your disposal", he responds.

Followed by his men, Yuri climbs into one of the waiting police cars of the mechanized division driving the unit to the waiting helicopters.

On the way to the helicopter he studies the floor plan of the building and the map of the town.

Before the police car of the mechanized division can stop in front of the waiting helicopters Yuri's men put on their bulletproof vests, harnesses, guns, knives, balaclavas and ready their headsets for the hostage rescue operation. They jump into one of the waiting helicopters.

Sergey is stopped by Yuri. He looks at him pointing on the map:

"Go on top of that roof! I need you to take one of the terrorists out of action. You've got 6 minutes from the moment you are on the roof. Use your silencer."

Sergey salutes: "Yes, Commander."

Sergey and two of the local policemen drive off.

The Head of Police hands Yuri his mobile phone. Yuri passes it to Dmitry. He jumps into the helicopter followed by Dmitry. The helicopter takes off.

7. The Sniper.

The terrorist on the roof of the school building sees the police cars in the street and, using his mobile, calls the terrorist-leader to come downstairs in the big hall, the second floor, where the hostages are kept:

"The police are gathering behind the building."

The terrorist leader answers: "I don't give a shit. Anyone from Spetsnaz?"

The terrorist on the roof responds:

"I don't see any."

The leader orders: "Keep watching!"

Sergey's masked face appears at the edge of the roof on the building opposite the school, and within seconds he is up, takes aim and a dull sound comes from the silenced gun.

Still holding his mobile, the terrorist slumps to the floor on the roof of the school. There is a bullet hole in his forehead.

8. Demons.

The helicopter with Yuri and his unit aboard flies up to the 3-story building behind the school complex.

Yuri looks at his watch, then announces to his men:

"I want this over and done within 8 minutes exactly!"

He and his men set their watches.

It is very hot in the big hall where the hostages are kept. The big windows are closed. The headmistress is still on her knees. She moves slightly:

"Please, we do need some water."

The terrorist-leader hits her on the head with the butt of his Kalashnikov:

"Shut up, you old bitch!"

The headmistress collapses to the ground. The terrorist-leader kicks her in her belly while checking the time on the clock on the wall. Only now he sees the thangka. Disgusted and raged he shouts:

"Demons!"

He points his machine gun at little Sveta and jabs her in the back:

"Turn around, pig face, and get the demon!"

The little girl is petrified. She looks at the young female teacher beside her for help. The young teacher is too scared to look at her and doesn't move.

The headmistress jumps to her feet, puts herself in front of Sveta and says to the terrorist-leader:

"It belongs to me. I will ..."

"Shut up, old bitch", the terrorist-leader shouts aggressively.

The thundering noise that sounds like a helicopter flying on the building is getting louder and louder and makes him hesitate for a moment as he is about to pull the trigger of his Kalashnikov. Instead, he grabs his mobile to call the terrorist on the roof. There is no response.

The terrorist-leader gets nervous. He yells at one of his henchmen to fetch the pig face and find out what is going on outside.

One of the terrorists grabs the petrified Sveta and uses her as a human shield dragging her to one of the big windows which looks out to the street.

Meanwhile, Yuri and his men fast-rope down onto the roof of the school building. They fix lines to the structure of the roof, fasten their harnesses and start to walk backwards very quickly down the walls of the school building.

Dmitry presses a few keys on his mobile phone. The terrorist-leader's phone rings. With a flash of rage he answers and shoots at the headmistress. The bullet grazes the headmistress's arm and she collapses to the floor once again.

Simultaneously Sergey takes aim of the terrorist standing at the window. A dull sound comes from the silenced gun. The glass of the window breaks. The terrorist slumps backwards to the floor. There is a bullet hole in his forehead.

Sveta is free. Without missing a beat she disappears behind the heavy window curtain.

More glass breaks. There is an explosion, a bright flash and a loud bang. Yuri and his men jump through the windows.

Yuri shoots the leader, who drops the mobile phone and collapses to the floor. There is confusion and fury among the terrorists. Yuri's men are shouting on top of their lungs: "Drop your weapons! Hands on your heads! Get on your knees. On the floor!"

The furious terrorists start to shoot at random. Two of them are hit by bullets coming from Dmitry's gun. Lifeless they fall to the floor. Another two are disarmed by Kirill and Andrey and their hands are tied. The firing stops.

Black bags are pulled over the heads of the surviving terrorists. One of the surviving terrorists cowers on the floor shivering. The smell of terror and urine permeates the air. He is crying like a child.

The head of the police, his men and the doctors run into the room.

"Five of the terrorists are dead, three are wounded. You can find them crying in the corner over there", Yuri says and points to the dead boy:

"This child was trying to escape. One woman is wounded."

9. No Bonds are Broken.

The children are gone from inside the big hall of the school build-ing. One of the doctors gives a signal to carry away Ivan's dead body covered by a plastic body bag. Ivan's father stares at his son's dead body while Ivan's mother cries in the arms of the headmistress. The headmistress' right arm is dressed and there is a bruise on the side of her face. She gently strokes the woman's hair and leads her to her husband.

The young female teacher from Murmansk can't stop crying. The other doctor gives her an injection to calm her down. The young female teacher confesses to the doctor with a tearful voice:

"I am so ashamed! I was a coward. I didn't help Sveta, I was so afraid of dying."

The headmistress approaches and with compassion says to the young teacher:

"Don't worry. Most people are afraid of death."

Yuri, still masked, enters the hall with Sveta, holding the girl's hand. The headmistress approaches Yuri and says:

"Thank you for saving our lives."

Yuri nods: "It looks like you are one of the few people I know who aren't afraid of dying. Sveta told me that you saved her life. They could have easily killed you. You must have a good protection." "Yes, Captain. I do."

The headmistress produces a plastic-coated photograph that she wears next to her heart and hands it to Yuri.

He takes a look at it. It shows a man with bright blue eyes, short blond hair and who looks very strong. Sveta, raising her eyes to Yuri, and asks:

"Do protectors always have blue eyes? I think they do." Still with the photograph in his hands, Yuri slowly takes off his mask. His bright blue eyes look first at Sveta and then at the headmistress who says smiling:

"This man brought back the religion of the Kalmucks that Stalin destroyed. He can protect you just as he protects me. He is a perennial protector."

Yuri answers firmly: "Perennial protector? I have this to protect me!"

He points at his gun and shows his bullet-proof vest.

The chief of the police approaches Yuri with his mobile phone in his hand: "Commander, the President would like a word."

Yuri nods and hands the photograph back to the headmistress. She stops him:

"Keep it, please. As a soldier you have no idea how long you will live."

Yuri's eyes catch the picture of Yama. He looks at it for a moment, thanks the headmistress and slides the photo in his pocket while answering the President's call.

A Sticky Affair

10. The video is designed to intimidate.

A car goes from Edinburgh, the capital city of Scotland, up a narrow road to a castle converted to a luxurious 5-star hotel. At the steering wheel is a young woman with short dark hair. Her name is Liz Crawford. Liz is a photographer and cameraman employed by FireWork International. She is wearing a pair of jeans, a t-shirt and worn-out sneakers.

Alba elegantly dressed sits beside her and is looking up to the castle: "Wow, what a location! The hotel with its towers, peaks and bays looks like like a fairy-tale castle." Liz smiles: "Yes, the Castle has seen much history and many kinds of fairy-tales. I was born a few steps from here. King Edward I (Longshanks) stayed at the castle on his way to meet Sir William Wallace at the Battle of Falkirk. In 1400, Sir Alexander Ramsay withstood a six-month siege at (Dalhousie) by English forces led by King Henry IV. Oliver Cromwell used the castle as a base for his invasion of Scotland. The castle is situated in a strategic spot overlooking the River Esk. The drum tower, the oldest part of the current structure, an L Plan Castle dates to the mid 15th century. It is magical and so is Scotland".

The car comes to a stop in front of a gate guarded by security personnel. Alba steps out. She shows their invitations to the Security. Alba and

Liz are asked to enter another car and are driven up to the castle. The big hall in the castle decorated with knights' amour, coats of arms and paintings of battle scenes on the walls is set up as a conference hall.

David Jefferson, an athletically built, tall blond American, in his late thirties delivers a speech to his audience. He stands in front of on old oak table and points to the screen on the wall. The other international experts on terrorism as well as the delegates and journalists are following David's speech with interest.

David requests: "Next slide please."

The picture shows the face of a dark skinned, long black bearded man with cold and lifeless dark eyes. He is in his early forties. David says: "The man you see on the screen is Ali Moussa. He is from Jordan. During the last 25 years he has killed hundreds, or possibly thousands of men, women, and children. He is a member of a worldwide network of terrorism and we know that they are focusing resources in Chechnya and that Ali Moussa is using the Caucasus as his base to direct their operations, their Holy War from there. There is also definitive evidence that Ali Moussa is connected with two terrorist acts in Africa where the US embassies were bombed in 1998."

David pauses for a moment before he goes on:

"He is extremely dangerous. Our expert on him and on his organisation is Captain Yuri Sokolov from Russia. The Captain will be joining us after lunch. He will arrive directly from Elista in Southern Russia, where he has recently rescued 250 schoolchildren and 6 teachers who were being held hostage by a group of 8 terrorists. Ali Moussa has claimed responsibility for this act."

The screen goes blank.

David tells his audience: "We'll take all your questions after lunch. See you in about an hour."

With a polite applause from the audience, the meeting adjourns.

Alba stands with a security guard in front of the closed door of the conference hall. Sounds of applause come from behind. The doors open. David steps out with a group of experts. The security guard approaches him. David looks at Alba, finishes his conversation and approaches her: "Hello, Mrs. Smith, I am David Jefferson. How's Steven?" Alba answers in a friendly way:

"Fortunately, his injuries are not too severe. He should be out of hospital in a couple of days."

Other experts walk by. David is tapped on his shoulder and congratulated on such a well-received event. A small group of Americans talk to him in the background. One of them says: "Well done, Dave!"

David nods gratefully, then notices a figure approaching. It's Yuri accompanied by Dmitry.

"Well, Mrs. Smith, I'm sorry but I have to excuse myself. Have a nice lunch and please join us for our afternoon program. I think it will be just perfect for your work."

David bows off and heads towards Yuri and Dmitry. Alba watches him. Alba and Yuri's eyes meet for a moment. David puts out his hand. "Captain Sokolov, Lieutenant Koval. Welcome to Scotland." The men shake hands.

"Major Jefferson, thank you for inviting us," Yuri replies. David inquires: "Is there any news from Moussa?"

"We have received a copy of a new video he is selling in Chechnya. It is designed to intimidate Russian soldiers," says Yuri. David is interested: "Do you think it would be suitable to show it to the press this afternoon?"

Alba slowly approaches the three men. Yuri watches her with one eye and answers:

"Well, many grown-up men have fainted watching it." Alba comes closer, smiling at Yuri:

"Excuse me for interrupting you. The material you are talking about might be of great interest for the feature I am working on."

David is not very pleased about the interruption but kindly explains to his Russian guests: "Miss Smith is an American journalist based in London. She's working on a series about terrorism". Alba specifies: "Actually I'm here looking for material to complete the pilot-episode. I'd like to know more about the video you mentioned."

For a second David looks at Yuri questioningly. Yuri states in a friendly way:

"We will be showing it later on. But first, I'd like to invite you to participate in one of our training sessions this afternoon."

"That sounds very exciting! Thanks for the invitation. I will be there", replies Alba with a radiant smile.

A Sticky Affair

11. I am ready for anything! I can do anything! I will endure anything!

Army tents are set up in a secluded area nearby the castle, the Hotel. A group of 30 American, English, German, French, Israeli, and Australian soldiers from Special Forces in combat gear warm up. They have applied camouflage on their faces, covered their hair with special head-scarves and wear their heavy equipment on the back.

Dmitry enters the scene providing the soldiers with written instructions for their task. He tells the soldiers:

"Read the provided instructions carefully. Start working right away."

Shortly afterwards Yuri arrives with another three men in uniforms. The soldiers form up in front of Yuri and the four officers.

Yuri greets the soldiers: "Good afternoon, everybody! I am Captain Sokolov. I will be leading this exercise with the assistance of Major Russell. Major Gutenberg, Major Bassett and Lieutenant Koval you have met already."

He points to Dmitry and continues: "Some parts of our training will be shown to the press later on. We intend to demonstrate how well we perform on a professional level in an international collaboration. Let's show everybody what we can do together."

Yuri raises his voice: "Repeat after me: I am ready for anything! I can do anything! I will endure anything!"

The entire squad starts to repeat the words in a focused manner:

"I am ready for anything! I can do anything! I will endure anything!"

Then Yuri announces: "You have exactly 1 hour and 45 minutes to fulfil your task. Good luck!"

The soldiers run off in two columns.

Meanwhile the delegates and journalists are driven in different jeeps from the castle down to the training camp to a parking area in front of a tent.

Alba sits next to a young man who introduces himself as Vladimir Dudkin, photographer and journalist for Ogonyok, in Moscow. Alba comes to know that Vladimir is the only Russian journalist invited to report in the Russian media about the international meeting of anti-terrorism experts. They exchange business cards.

David and a group of other experts are in the tent ready for the afternoon program. As soon as the last ones of the group of the delegates and journalists have entered the tent, David motions to everybody to sit down:

"We will start the afternoon program with some clips of terrorist acts carried out by extremist organisations."

Everybody turns to the screen. David starts to comment on the documentary:

"October 19, 1994. A powerful bomb, apparently placed by a militant faction opposed to the Arab-Israeli peace negotiations, blew up a crowded bus during the morning rush hours in the heart of Tel Aviv, Israel, killing 22 people and wounding 48.

July 18, 1994. A huge bomb placed by an extremist group exploded destroying a seven-story down-town building housing two Jewish groups in Buenos Aires, Argentina. At least 26 people were killed and 127 were injured.

February 26, 1993. A tremendous underground explosion believed to be caused by a bomb placed by a terrorist network, shook the 110-story twin towers of Manhattan's World Trade Center, in New York killing at least five people, injuring more than 1000, and sending tens of thousands of workers fleeing for their lives down crowded smoke-filled stairs.

May 4, 1992. 13 Egyptian Christians were shot dead by fundamentalists in Mansheit Nasser, Egypt. Ten Christian farmers were ambushed and murdered while working in their fields. A Christian teacher was shot in a local school while teaching a class of ten-year olds. A Christian doctor was shot outside his home."

The screen goes black.

David remarks: "These are just a few examples of thousands of terrorist attacks all over the world."

"It seems that violence committed by certain extremists far exceeds that of other groups. Major Jefferson. Why do you think they behave in such a way," Vladimir addresses himself to David.

"To understand the motivation of different groups we need to understand the teachings that they follow. There are religions that advocate the killing of those whose views differ from their own. In certain circumstances this can lead to Holy Wars. In the case of a Holy War, those people who die for their cause are promised a life in a paradise and they do not believe that they are maliciously hurting others, but rather obeying the words of their Gods," David explains.

An officer in uniform enters. He speaks for a moment to David. David nods and continues: "Now, to our next point of the agenda: We have organised a training exercise with a group of soldiers from a variety of special-ops task forces for you all to observe." Alba raises her hand: "Yes, Miss Smith?"

"What's the reason for this exercise,"Alba inquires.

"Terrorism is no longer the problem of just one nation any more. It has become an international problem, a problem of the free world. Therefore, governments have started to work together more closely and have decided to share intelligence and information. This sharing also includes the Special Forces, who exchange experience and methods to be able to protect our freedom.

There may soon be a possibility, in fact a very real need, for such an international anti-terrorist squad," David responds.

"And how would such a task force function," Alba asks.

"The same way that Delta or any other Special Forces services function in the world. But this one would act solely in response to UN mandates".David looks at his watch: "Well, our soldiers have finished the first part of the exercise. The cars are ready to bring you to up to the cliff to follow the second part."

12. Perfect Weapons.

Alba, Liz and the other journalists are led up to the top of a cliff. Alba steps towards the edge of the cliff and looks down. She turns around to Liz holding her stomach: "I always feel sick when I look down like that." Liz looks over and nods.

The soldiers are approaching. They are heavily armed and covered in mud. Now their painted faces have a war expression on them. Some of them are bleeding from their noses. Liz and the other cameramen get ready to film.

Yuri appears. His eyes and Alba's meet for a second once again. Yuri orders the soldiers:

"You will do 500 squats, then spin around 300 times. Put your climbing gear on, fast rope down as quickly as possible and run to the boats waiting for you. Be aware that the enemy could strike any time. Your life and the lives of the hostages are on the line!"

Yuri holds his hand up, signals to them to prepare, pulls his hand down and shouts: "GO!"

The soldiers then quickly break up into two groups, put their climbing gear on and check each other's equipment. One of the soldiers tells another one to tie his shoelaces of his right boot. Then they form up in two lines, do the required repetitions of squats and spins, take the ropes, tie them around their bodies and fast rope down the cliff.

The delegates and journalists are taken down to the riverside. They arrive just in time to see the last soldiers coming down the cliff. Now everything happens very fast. As soon as the soldiers have reached the shore they run to the boats. Yuri and the other senior men start running beside the soldiers.

Yuri shouts: "Take the boats, run to the water and paddle 1 km out. Turn around and come back to the shore again."

Yuri looks at his watch: "You are still in time. For every minute longer a hostage will be killed and that is your responsibility. Do you want to be responsible for the deaths of women and children? Go, go, go!"

The soldiers lift the boats onto their shoulders, run to the beach, throw the boats in the water and climb into them. Suddenly masked men emerge from the water around them. Hand to hand fighting breaks out between the two groups. The international team works well together, disarming their opponents while protecting each other.

Alba, absorbed by the performance of the soldiers, suddenly feels something close by. She turns around. Yuri is standing beside her.

Alba says impressively: "That looks like pure torture. How can their bodies stand such extremes?"

Yuri answers: "The body has to be trained in this way. It is the most precious tool we have for protecting others. Otherwise we would die and the hostages would certainly also die. Our aim is to make the men invulnerable, so that they will become perfect weapons."

"Perfect weapons...."Alba pensively says.

"Yes. Eventually, everything is very simple," Yuri responds.

The soldiers arrive at the shore. Yuri smiles at Alba, then he walks to the soldiers. He commands:

"Now do another 100 squats with your trainer inside the boats. After that, climb back up the cliff."

The trainers jump into the boats and the men lift them up.

13. How does it feel to be a hostage?

The press and delegates are picked up and driven to an old ruined house. Yuri appears and steps in front of the press and the delegates: "At the end of the training, after all the physical exertion, the soldiers will now liberate some hostages. Please follow me."

The group enters the decayed building. Inside there is a large dusty hall with several broken windows and a majestic but dilapidated staircase that leads to the upper floors. As soon as everybody has entered the hall Yuri points to five masked and armed men at the back of the hall: "These are criminals who have taken some hostages. Now we need six people who would volunteer to be the hostages."

Yuri looks around. Three men and two women step forward. One of the men is Vladimir. Alba notices that Vladimir nods to Yuri with a friendly smile which Yuri returns before he looks around asking:

"We need one more hostage. Miss Smith. How about you?" Alba takes a peek at the masked and armed men and at Vladimir and agrees:

"Sure, why not?"

Yuri points at a dark corner of the dusty hall: "The five of you, please walk to the corner". Yuri turns to Alba:

"Miss Smith, please stay with me."

The five hostages walk over to the corner of the hall whereas the remaining delegates and journalists are directed up the stairs to watch from the balcony. Alba stands beside Yuri who observes everything. He turns to the five hostages:

"Sit down. Avoid every eye contact with the criminals. Stay down with your head slightly bowed."

Yuri says to Alba: "Miss Smith, please come with me." Yuri guides Alba a couple of steps down to a room, which leads into the basement. A masked criminal is standing there. The press and delegates look at Yuri, Alba and the masked criminal with interest.

Yuri pointing at the masked man explains to the audience:

"This criminal will use Miss Smith as his living shield. Miss Smith, do you mind?" Alba replies nervously:

"No problem. Just as long as I don't get shot."

The masked criminal quickly grabs Alba, and holds her head in his left arm. Alba can't move. She looks uncomfortable. Yuri leaves. The masked criminal touches Alba's hair and remarks to the audience:

"Nice hair."

The hostages are now on their knees with their heads down, looking towards the dirty wall. The criminals point their guns towards them. Liz and the other camera operator start to film from the balcony.

Outside the run-down building six masked hostage rescuers are ready for the hostage-freeing operation.

Yuri puts on his black balaclava and gives some signals to his men. Three of them make a staircase with their bodies in front of one of the broken windows. The other ones get ready to jump over them and into the building.

There is a big bang. A canister is thrown through the window and covers some of the room with smoke. The audience looks a little shocked. The hostage rescuers jump through the broken window, one following the other, into the hall. Very loud shouting comes from the hostage rescuers. Shots ring out from both sides of the combatants.

The rescuer with brilliant blue eyes, runs towards the staircase leading down to where Alba is being held. The masked criminal reaches for his knife and holds it at Alba's throat. Alba becomes very nervous but keeps looking at her rescuer. In a fraction of a second he jumps high and flies through space towards the criminal, he grabs hold of the knife and hits the criminal on the throat with his foot, pushing Alba behind him at the same time. The criminal falls to the ground. The rescuer takes out a sackcloth and pulls it over the criminal's head.

Slowly, Yuri takes his mask off. Alba sits on the ground trembling. Their eyes meet. He reaches for her, takes her in his arms and holds her tightly, asking:

"Are you okay?"

Alba is shaking in Yuri's arms: "Yes. I think so. You are with me!" Alba is smiling at him in gratitude and continues: "What an experience! It all seemed so real! Thanks." Alba takes a deep breath:

"Being taken as a hostage must be one of the worst experiences in life."

"Well", Yuri says, "most of the people who have been taken hostage can't live a normal life anymore."

Yuri asks Alba to follow him. Upstairs, smoke still fills the air. The criminals are lying on the ground. Their hands are tied and sack-cloths are pulled over their heads. The cameramen of the press of the different TV Stations and news-magazines are still taking pictures.

Yuri beckons to the press and the delegates to follow him.

Outside, the soldiers acting as rescuers are waiting for Yuri at parade rest. Their faces show both excitement and fatigue. Yuri happily addresses them:

"I am very proud of all of you! You made it once again. Congratulations! Your timing was excellent. The hostages are safe. The terrorists are in the hands of the authorities. You are a good team. Well done. Go and get cleaned up."

The soldiers smile, turn and head toward the showers.

14. The Cruel Footage.

Yuri stands behind the big table in the conference hall with a screen behind him. The other experts are alongside him with the delegates and journalists seated facing them. Yuri explains to the audience:

"What we are about to show you now concerns one of the most prolific terrorists operating at the moment. His name is Ali Moussa, but he uses a number of different aliases", Yuri pauses for a moment:

"Many people have had problems with the footage and have been unable to watch it. If you don't think you can watch the film, please feel free to leave the room. The video contains some extremely violent and cruel footage and it will leave some hard to digest impressions in your mind. There will be no problem if you decide not to participate and we will welcome you back into the hall afterwards."

Yuri looks around. No one leaves. Yuri asks for the video to be started.

Ali Moussa appears on the screen. He is wearing a modern uniform and holds a Kalashnikov. In front of him stand a group of mostly young long-bearded and dark-skinned males. Many of them are still only boys.

30 heavily armed bodyguards who are masked surround Ali. At a distance of 15 meters, 20 men in Russian uniforms are chained to poles. Ali yells in the direction of the young dark-skinned males:

"Mujahideen! What is the greatest deed one can do other than to believe in God?"

The young males shout: "To fight in a Holy War, for his cause.""

Ali continues: "Mujahideen! Everyone who participates in a Holy War, when not compelled to do so except for his belief in God, will be rewarded by him either here or be admitted to paradise if he is martyred."

Ali points to the Russian prisoners and orders:

"Strike terror into the hearts of the enemies of God and into the hearts of your enemies!"

He raises his Kalashnikov. All the others lift their rifles as well and shout: "God is great!"

Ali walks slowly along the row of young dark-skinned men. He grasps a slightly puny looking one and forces a knife into his hand: "Mujahideen, come along!"

Ali and the young man approach one of the chained Russians. A deep wound is gaping across his face. The prisoner can hardly keep his head straight. Ali pushes the Russian's head to the side, showing his throat.

He turns to the young men who are eagerly observing the scene, raise their Kalashnikovs and again shout:

"God is great!"

Ali runs his eye down the row:

"Mujahideen, this is the throat of a prisoner."

He smiles into the camera, holding the heavily wounded Russian by his head. Then he looks at the young man to the side whose eyes glitter feverishly:

"Kill him, and God will punish him by your hands, cover him with shame. Cut his throat!"

Alba turns her head away from the screen and covers her eyes. Liz looks at her, a worried expression on her face. Alba hears Ali shout:

"God will instil terror into the hearts of the unbelievers, smash everything above their necks and crush their fingertips. It is not you who slays them, it is God who slays them."

Alba gets up, heading toward the big door without looking at the screen. Yuri looks over at her, then back to the screen.

The young jihadists jump up. They keep their rifles high, run towards the Russian prisoners, thrust their bayonets again and again into the stomachs of their enemies.

Ali looks with approval at his men: "God is great! What a day!"

After having carried out the massacre, the young jihadists fall into two lines with their weapons slung over their shoulders and walk away.

On their way back to a run-down wooden building they see posters of a long-bearded man with a white turban which are pasted everywhere.

15 A million dollars on my head.

There is complete silence in the room. For a moment the delegates and the journalists remain in a state of shock.

Yuri gets up from the table: "Still today, Ali Moussa and his followers use live targets to train their soldiers in cruelty. As you can see, it is our men that they use. Moussa's videos are not only sold to intimidate our army but also to prove how many men they have killed or taken hostage during an attack. They are paid for each man they kill or take prisoner. For example a Russian army general is worth forty bulls, a major sixty rams. For Special task officers like Spetsnaz they pay even more.

I am honoured to have a price tag of a million dollars on my head. Russian army officers are usually exchanged for their captured fighters. But Spetsnaz officers are always tortured and then killed. Terrorists pay large sums of money for foreign mercenaries and instructors. The mercenaries are often recruited in London and other places in the West. The instructors come mainly from Pakistan, Egypt and Afghanistan, but they also have Russian instructors."

Yuri pauses for a moment before going on:

"That is very difficult for us to understand. Do you have any questions?"

A German journalist gets up: "Captain Sokolov, what role does Ali Moussa play in the Chechen war?"

"He plays a leading role. He is responsible not only for organizing the war in Chechnya, but for personally carrying out hundreds of atrocities against the Russian army and against the Chechen people. To put it quite simply, he is a terrorist", Yuri answers the question.

A journalist from Italy comes up with a question: "Captain Sokolov, how is it possible that these terrorists can train their people in Russia?"

"The Caucasus is a very convenient location – mountainous and isolated", Yuri explains.

The Italian journalist continues: "What else can you tell us about their training program?"

"Well, it's quite cruel but effective. If recruits shoot off target once, they are punished with twenty or thirty lashings on the soles of their feet. It is a very rigid structure. Very often people think that terrorists are like a flock of sheep. That is a mistake. They have a very well organised hierarchy and are very disciplined."

The next question comes from a woman journalist from Austria: "Captain, what different types of training do they receive?"

"They are taught subversion tactics, the details of guerilla warfare, marksmanship, and psychological training. I could go on and on. The only thing they can't do in the Caucasus is parachute jumping because the terrain is too inhospitable. They copy the methods used successfully both within Russia and abroad. A recent bombing of a railway in Chechnya closely mimicked one from France. They also show their recruits films with scenes from funerals of former fighters. They show how their coffins are carried on the shoulders of other potential martyrs, through the town where they came from. They celebrate them as heroes and the highest clerics and generals are present to honour the martyr's families", Yuri lists up. "Any last questions, please."

Vladimir stands up: "Captain, is there a possibility to capture this criminal?"

Yuri looks directly at Vladimir: "Yes. There is always such a possibility."

16. We share the same values.

Alba sits at the table in the dining room of the castle. The tables are set for dinner. She looks pale, is far away in her thoughts and occasionally sips from a cup of peppermint tea.

Yuri approaches: "May I join you?" Alba looks up, into Yuri's face: "Yes, of course."

Yuri sits down. Alba says: "Err.. they have some nice drinks at the bar. Can I get you something before dinner? What would you like?"

"Actually, I haven't touched alcohol for years. An espresso would be fine", Yuri declines.

A waiter comes to the table. He asks Alba and Yuri what he can get them. Alba notices a familiar accent. His name badge reads Gaetano Fantuzzi. Alba orders in Italian. The waiter takes the order and leaves a bit surprised.

"Your Italian is very good", Yuri remarks.

Alba smiles: "Thanks. I am half Italian and half American. Actually the only thing that makes me American is my passport because I was born in New York."

Yuri concludes: "That means that you grew up in Italy." Alba happily confirms: "Yes, that's right. We moved back to Italy where my mother comes from, when I was one year old. My dad was offered to work for NCI in Rome. It's an Italian petroleum company, with advanced technology and lots of rich Saudis. They're my dad's clients and business partners. My dad made good money with them. We lived a good life but my mom was always uncomfortable with the people my dad had to deal with. In particular she was very disturbed about how they treat their women and violate human rights. In the end my mom left my dad."

"Your mom seems to have different values than your dad", Yuri states.

"Well, it seems to be so. They come from different worlds. My dad comes from a very poor and numerous family. There were twelve children. He was the oldest. When his father died, he was only 16 years old and he became the head of the family. He had to take care of his brothers and sisters and his mom. He left school and started to work. Money was always and still is a big issue in my dad`s life although he is a rich man. Now he has the problem of keeping it and not losing it."

Alba smiles and pauses for a moment before she continues: "Maybe I am talking too much and boring you with my family stories. There are many more important topics we could talk about."

"You are not boring me at all", Yuri says kindly. He looks at Alba and asks: "What about your mom from which world as you say, does she come from?"

"The world my mom comes from is a world of kindness, empathy, knowledge, compassion, courage, beauty, idealism. She is the only daughter of an old aristocratic family in Florence. During the Second World War, my grandmother, back then a young woman saved many peoples´ lives risking her own. She is a hero. She always sets an example for me."

"She is still alive", Yuri inquires. Alba nods happily:

"Yes, she is and she lives in her beautiful 17th century villa outside of Florence."

"My grandmother was Jewish", Yuri says, "under the regime of Stalin she and her family were deported to one of Stalin's gulags. There she met a high ranking officer, Yuri Orlow, whom she fell in love with, my grandfather. He played a dual role in the gulag. Actually, he belonged to the resistance and saved many peoples' lives, among others also my grandmother's. He helped her escape the gulag and he hid her in the house of a doctor and his wife who also belonged to the resistance. A couple of weeks later my grandmother gave birth to a little girl, my mother, in the house of the doctor. Unfortunately grandmother died seven days after my mother was born. My mother was told when she was a teenager that her mother died because she was deeply shocked when she came to know that her beloved Yuri was executed for treason on the day my mother was born."

Alba touches Yuri's arm gently: "That is a very sad story. And what happened to your mom?"

Yuri sighs: "She was brought up by the doctor and his wife. They loved her like the child they never had. My mother became a doctor as well. She died one year ago."

"You loved your mom very much", says Alba.

"Yes. She was a remarkable woman and a great doctor. She helped so many women, especially those who have experienced physical and psychological violence."

"Did she experience violence herself", Alba asks. Yuri reflects before continuing: "She had a very happy childhood and was loved very much by the doctor and his wife. However my father did not treat her well. He used to be very violent. But she was lucky and left him just in time." Alba says with tears in her eyes:

"Women are so vulnerable and are worth nothing still today. Domestic violence and other forms of violence against women are more common than one thinks and widespread especially in underdeveloped theocratic countries and rural parts of the world. My mom has stood up for women's rights and I would like to help as well."

"Why don't you do it? Your are a journalist", Yuri remarks with a provoking look. Alba kindly asks:

"Were you abused by your father?"

Yuri takes Alba's hand and holds it for a moment:

"Yes, when I tried to protect my mom. Back then I decided to learn how to protect others. I found a martial arts teacher, trained hard and eventually became a national champion. The GRU heard about me and I was brought to a camp in Kazakhstan where I was trained to become a Spetsnaz officer."

"It seems that we all have a task to fulfil: We both use our human potential. You as a soldier and a perfect weapon....", Alba smiles at him before she continues, "you protect our freedom, the weak and children. As for me, being a journalist who is educated and aware of what is going on in the world, I have the task of protecting freedom of speech."

"Yes, we belong to the same family. We share the same values", says Yuri. Alba nods.

The waiter brings the espresso for Yuri and a drink for Alba. Yuri looks interested at Alba's drink: "You seem to be feeling better"..

"Yes, I feel much better." Alba looks squarely into Yuri's eyes: "Please, could you teach me how to protect myself and others?"

"Certainly I can teach you how to protect yourself and others. Come to Russia and I'll teach you very sufficient and fast methods."

"I'll take you up on it!" Alba says.

"It is a pleasure for me. By the way, what are you drinking?"

"This is called a Bellini", Alba responds, "crushed fresh peaches and a little bit of champagne. It always reminds me of a wonderful and happy time in Rome and my first love. He was a Carabiniere. He was shot. He was only 28 years old. He died on duty."

"I am sorry. That's too early to die", Yuri answers."

"Maybe I've just become a little bit too sentimental. Let's go back to work. I have a question to ask you", Alba suggests.

"Ok, please do."

"Captain, how do you deal with terrorism, torture, killing, dying?"

The dining hall slowly fills up with members of the press and the delegates.

"You don't deal with it. It's hell. It's as simple as that. You can't allow yourself to think about it", Yuri answers.

"I understand. By the way would you leave the tape for us, to use it in our pilot-film?"

Yuri thinks for a moment, then looks at Alba: "I don't think it's a good idea to leave the tape. Not at this time."

"And what about an interview later on this evening", Alba asks. Before Yuri can answer the question Dmitry approaches Yuri. He is with Liz. Dmitry greets Alba and says something urgently to his commander in Russian. Yuri stands up: "Duty calls. We have to leave. I'm sorry about the interview. Let's talk again in two weeks time in St. Petersburg."

For one moment Yuri gently touches Alba's arm. Alba inquires:

"How will I find you?"

"Oh, don't worry about that. I will find you", Yuri grins.

"Sure", Alba laughs. She reaches into her bag and pulls out the new mobile phone, supposed to be her mom's birthday gift. Alba offers it to him with a twinkle in her eyes: "Here. Please take this. It will connect us all over the world. You will find me and I will find you."

Yuri hesitates, not sure what to do. Alba reassures him:

"You can give it back to me when we meet again."

Yuri smiles, and takes it: "All right. Why not? Thanks."

On the way out of the dining room Yuri turns around a last time to Alba: "See you and Liz in St. Petersburg."

Alba smiles happily.

17. Let's join the adventure.

As soon as Yuri and Dmitry have left the dining room Liz takes Yuri's place at Alba's table. She takes out a cigarette, lights it and looks at Alba: "Do you like him?"

Alba answers with a great smile on her face:

"Yes, I do. He is very special. In some ways he reminds me of my first love, Lorenzo. He was a noble Italian from Florence like my mom."

"Well, Yuri might not be noble by birth, nevertheless he has a noble and brave heart", says Liz.

"Yes, that's true. And what about you? It seems to me you are in love with Dmitry."

Liz beams: "Yes, you're right. It was love at first sight." Alba hugs Liz: "One can see that. You look very happy. Dmitry is a very good- looking man. Blond and tall."

Alba pauses for a moment; with a twinkle in her eyes she continues: "He is just the opposite of Yuri."

Liz remarks: "But Dmitry is not the commander, the man in charge. You would never go for the second in command."

"Well, it does seem that I am drawn to leaders", Alba laughs. Liz nods in agreement.

Alba changes the subject. "So, what about going to St. Petersburg like Yuri suggested? He might be willing to give us an interview as well as provide us with the tape of the cruel footage we recently saw."

Liz agrees instantly: "I am ready. What are you waiting for?"

"Well, we have a couple of hindrances to overcome. This is Steven's project. My job here is over, so I'll have to go back to London and work on The Rich & Famous, and that applies to you too", Alba smiles at Liz.

"I don't think that it will be so difficult. It's you the Captain trusts, not Steven. So, you're the only one who can get the interview and the tape. Without both, the series won't be successful", Liz states. Alba nods:

"I think you're right. But we both know that Cynthia won't put The Rich & Famous on hold for two weeks."

"Maybe we can speed up the project to get the stuff we need and follow the Captain to his next assignment. Even if this should take us to Chechnya."

Alba is aghast: "What do you mean? You want to follow him to the war?"

"Exactly. Can you think of some other way to get the footage as fast?"

"Well, there we'd get more authentic material for sure. Although it won't be a walk in the park. Cynthia would not hesitate to send us to the war to get sensational news to ensure high viewing figures!" Liz nods.

"The key to get what we want is Cynthia's greed."

Alba laughs: "OK. Let's join the adventure!"

A Sticky Affair

18. Just keep your hands out of my business.

Khankala is a settlement in Groznensky District of the Chechen Republic, Russia, located to the east of Grozny, the republic's capital. It is the location of a Russian military base, the headquarters of the 42nd Motor Rifle Division, and an airstrip at the eastern outskirts of Grozny, also overtaking the main Rostov-Baku highway and cutting direct access into the Chechen capital of Grozny from the town of Argun.

A group of tanks crawl down the hill. Orders are shouted in Russian. Children play between young soldiers who are busy packing. A military helicopter lands.

Yuri and his men emerge weighed down by their heavy equipment.

The Adjutant General knocks at the door of a small wooden building. There is no response, so he tries to open the door. Since it's locked, he calls: "General, we have visitors. The Spetsnaz unit have just arrived."

Yuri heads for the office of the General and salutes the Adjutant General: "Captain Sokolov reporting for duty."

The door opens and a General steps out. His uniform is slightly disordered and his speech is slurred:

"Captain Sokolov, you are early. We didn't expect you until this evening."

Yuri replies: "General Korsakov, we have arrived just in time."

A young woman sneaks out of the office. Yuri notices but doesn't react. Yuri reports:

"Our orders are to escort the convoy to Gudermes tomorrow."

"That's exactly what I wanted to talk to you about. Please come in."

The General's office is in a state of advanced disorder.

He takes two glasses and a bottle of vodka out of a cupboard, fills both glasses and puts one of them in front of Yuri: "Captain, to your health."

The general drinks, Yuri doesn't.

General Korsakov rumbles: "Of course! I forgot. You don't have such vices. You are a man of honour. You remember your first medal? You know you got that because of me, don't you?"

"General. We're here to secure the convoy and do some scouting at the front."

General Korsakov does not seem to have heard Yuri and says: "22 years ago, I was the youngest and most promising General in the Russian army. Then, the Mujahedeen took me hostage. If I remember correctly, it was because of you that I was freed. Did you get the Red Beret for this?"

"General, the terrorist Mustafa ben Ammar was exchanged for you and General Chevalkov."

The General pensively says: "Is that true? It was Ammar?"

He pauses for a moment before he continues in a commanding tone:"Well, we took care of the scouting already and there are more than enough men in the convoy."

The General pours another shot of vodka in his glass and drinks. Yuri insists: "General, an order is an order."

General Korsakov sternly states:

"Captain, we, the Russian army, have the situation under control. Be our guests, relax and have some fun. Sometimes during war, such short breaks are necessary."

The General stands: "You are dismissed."

Yuri stands as well, salutes and leaves the room.

The General takes Yuri's glass and downs the vodka in one swallow. He mutters: "Just keep your hands out of my business."

19. Politics is dirty business.

Pensively, Yuri walks back to his unit, smoking a cigarette. His men are gathered around a group of young soldiers. A young soldier happily says to Yuri's men:

"We made it. For us, this war is over. We're leaving. We're going home!"

The other young soldiers nod in agreement:

"The convoy is due to leave very early tomorrow morning. In four days I will see my girlfriend, at home in Novosibirsk."

Yuri signs for his men to follow him.

At a safe distance to the young soldiers he informs his men about the General's decision:

"By the General's orders, we are not going to escort the convoy tomorrow. He has been so generous to grant us some days of vacation in his health resort instead."

In the background, the General leaves his office having problems walking in a straight line.

Mikhail complains: "We could have finished this war in two weeks!"

Yuri just shrugs his shoulders: "Politics is dirty business." Sergey approaches Yuri: "Captain, this is my first assignment. I need some experience. Could I sneak into the convoy and keep an eye on the soldiers?"

"When I was your age I assigned myself to a similar mission. Got me into a lot of trouble."

Sergey insists: "But Captain, may I remind you that you not only survived, but that this experience made you even stronger."

Yuri looks at Sergey's determined face. He shortly remarks: "They leave early tomorrow morning."

20. A helper on the way.

The Mozdok military air basis is a huge tent city with roughly 3,000 tents, 114 mess halls, shower and bath units and vehicle wash bays. It is early morning.

The sound of distant shooting and the roar of artillery fire fill the air. The camp awakens. Soldiers in ruined old uniforms emerge from their tents. They make themselves some tea and open cans of food.

Alba and Liz gather with other journalists, mostly Russians, in a run-down waiting room. Many of them are smoking.

A Russian journalist offers Alba and Liz cigarettes. Liz thanks the man and takes one. Alba also thanks him but refuses. The man asks Alba: "Do you mind if I smoke?" Alba smiles: "Not today. It only bothers me when I have a headache."

The Russian lights his cigarette asking:

"Where do you come from?"

"We are from London", Liz answers.

He continues asking:

"And what are you doing here? This is a strange place to visit for such beautiful women."

Liz responds: "We are journalists, we are working on a TV-series about terrorism."

Alba interferes:

"Are you a journalist?"

"Yes, I am a war correspondent."

The war correspondent pauses for a moment before he continues: "You're looking for Spetsnaz officers? Here at the front?"

Alba does not respond and looks at her watch. The war correspondent insists: "Maybe I can help you. Come with me to Khankala. Spetsnaz units are often based there, before they leave for missions in the Caucasus. I'm going there today."

"Thanks a lot for your kind offer", Alba says, "but we'll be meeting our guide shortly".

In that moment Vladimir enters with a great smile on his face. He greets Alba and Liz. When Vladimir discovers the war correspondent the smile on his face disappears. Nevertheless, he greets him politely.

At the same time in Khankala HQ a military truck sounds its horn. Wheels dig into the mud. The convoy starts moving and heads towards the rising sun, in the direction Yuri and his men are looking. Yuri stands in front of a tent holding a cup of hot tea. Sergey is sitting on the back of the first tank. He secretly salutes as he passes by. Yuri nods, then grabs the headphones and puts them on.

21 The Ambush.

The army convoy drives through a beautiful rolling landscape over a small dusty and winding road. Birds are singing and the atmosphere is peaceful. Although the noise the tanks are creating is deafening, Sergey suddenly notices that the birds have stopped singing. Sergey radios Yuri:

"Captain, something strange has just happened. The birds have stopped singing."

Yuri orders urgently: "Get off the tank immediately!"

Mines explode. The first and the last tank of the convoy disintegrate. The convoy comes to a stop. Then all the other tanks explode one after the other. Yuri hears the explosion through the headphones:

"Sergey!"

Yuri shouts into the radio. He gets no answer and tries again:

"Sergey!"

Yuri throws down the headphones and jumps to his feet:

"The convoy has been attacked. Start the helicopter and get the ambulance!"

There's fire, heat, smoke, body-parts and pieces of metal are flying around, inhuman cries of pain and desperation ring out. Soldiers try to escape bullets raining down from the hills. Heavily armed men with dark bearded faces and camouflage scarves around their heads run down the hills from all directions. They are shouting: "God is great! God is great!"

After the explosions stop, Ali Moussa appears. He is surrounded by his bodyguards and a cameraman.

Moussa lets himself be filmed as he walks around the scene. He starts kicking the dead and seriously injured soldiers lying on the ground. His bodyguards do the same. Methodically, they put soldiers who are still alive in front of the camera and kill them by cutting their throats.

The young Russian soldiers who have to watch the carnage are horrified. One of Moussa's bodyguards rips the guts of a soldier out of his stomach, holds them high and shouts: "God is great! God is great!"

Satisfied, Moussa walks around this place of horror protected by his bodyguards. He makes sure that none of the enemy soldiers are still alive. From time to time he or one of his bodyguards fires his Kalashnikov into the body of a dying Russian soldier.

In front of the camera, he proudly points to what is left of the destroyed tanks, and explains that the unidentifiable chunks of bloody meat around him were once Russian soldiers.

Motionless, Sergey lies in the bushes next to the burnt-out tank. Blood drips from his head. His right arm is seriously burnt. Sergey can see how Ali's henchmen finish off the wounded soldiers. Moussa comes closer and orders: "Go get the weapons and ammunition."

A group of Moussa's henchmen leave and walk to one of the trucks that wasn't demolished.

Sergey reaches for his knife and remains lifeless while Moussa and one of his bodyguards get closer to him.

The instant Moussa kicks Sergey, he jumps up and stabs Moussa in his chest with the knife. The bodyguard shoots and hits Sergey. Both Moussa and Sergey fall to the ground. Suddenly, there's the sound of helicopters in the background. Confusion and shouting arise.

"Spetsnaz are coming", one of the terrorists yells.

The bodyguard drags off his leader and escapes with the rest of the criminals.

A Sticky Affair

22. What did you expect? A helicopter ride?

Alba, Liz and Vladimir climb in the back of a dilapidated old car. Alba indignantly asks Vladimir: "That's what they call safe transportation?"

In the front of the car, next to the car driver sits a Russian farmer woman with a rooster in a cage on her lap.

The driver explains in Russian that the lady is his mother and he is bringing her to the next village which they will pass by anyway.

Vladimir translates for Alba and Liz. Alba says to Vladimir: "Please tell him it's okay, but is he sure the car will make it to Khankala?"

The driver smiles at Alba and asks Vladimir to translate that Alba and her friend shouldn't worry, the car will make it not only to Khankala but also to Moscow.

Alba is not really convinced. At that reaction, Vladimir laughs: "What did you expect? A helicopter ride?"

"Yes, that's exactly what I expected, especially when I consider the price we have just paid", says Alba in a serious tone and continues with a radiant smile:

"Although it is not a helicopter, you are a great friend. Thanks a lot for arranging everything and coming with us into the lion's den."

23. I will kill him I promise.

The rising sun radiates like a mountain of countless rubies. Yuri, Dmitry and Mikhail find Sergey still lying in the bushes. He is bleeding heavily.

Yuri kneels beside Sergey. He opens his eyes and looks at Yuri with a smile on his face:

"Commander, I knew you would make it!"

Yuri gently orders: "Don't talk, Sergey!"

He turns to Dmitry and Mikhail: "We have to stop the bleeding."

Dmitry and Mikhail take out their medical packs and start to tend to Sergey's wounds. Sergey reports to Yuri:

"It was a trap. It was a gun-running deal gone bad. They slaughtered them all like sheep. It was Ali. I got him with the knife. His men carried him away."

Yuri states with an ice-cold expression on his face:

"I will kill him, I promise!"

Sergey reaches for Yuri's hand: "I am dying. I'm afraid."

Sergey can't see clearly anymore. He floats between consciousness and unconsciousness.

On impulse, Yuri digs his free hand into the breast pocket of his uniform and takes out the photograph of the blond-haired man the headmistress of the school had given him what seems a lifetime ago. He presses it gently to Sergey's heart: "Don't be afraid, Sergey. You are a warrior."

In a gentle but firm voice, Yuri chants:

"You are ready for anything. You can do anything. You will endure anything."

Sergey says with a smile on his face: "My commander..."

Sergey makes three final drawn-out exhalations.

Yuri, Dmitry, and Mikhail look at each other with a deep sadness in their eyes. With tears in his eyes, Yuri closes Sergey's eyes.

24. The Gun-Running Deal.

Yuri is back in the HQ of Khankala and stands behind a tent with Alba's mobile phone on his ear. He says something in Russian and switches it off.

The Adjutant General attended by the war correspondent approach from behind. He looks suspiciously at the mobile: "Captain, I was looking for you. You are not to go and hunt down the terrorists. Here is an order for you to show up in Mozdok, immediately. A helicopter is ready to bring you and your unit there. Comrade Saizew, our war correspondent from Moscow is coming with you. Maybe you would like to tell him something about the death of one of your men."

Yuri ignores the war correspondent and continues in a cold voice: "Who is doing the job, the army again?"

The Adjutant General cuts Yuri off: "Captain, we both made a mistake. As you know an order is still an order."

The two men salute each other.

In the background, there is the sound of a helicopter drawing closer.

25. Everything is under control.

The ad-lib taxi with Alba, Liz and Vladimir is stopped on its way to Khan-kala military air base by three Russian soldiers with their Kalashnikovs at the ready.

Smoke rises from behind the hills. One of the soldiers orders the driver and Vladimir to get out of the car. The driver and Vladimir step out. Alba is about to do the same but immediately stopped by a second soldier who shouts at Alba to stay in the car. Appalled by the aggressive soldier Alba sits down in the back of the car beside Liz again. The two women don't talk but look at each other. Although they don't understand what the soldier is telling the driver and Vladimir, it is quite evident that something serious must be happening.

As soon as the two men are back in the car and they are out of the soldier's sight, Alba turns to Vladimir who is sitting beside the driver now just after the driver's mother has left the car in the middle of the way at Khankala.

Alba asks Vladimir curiously: "What happened? Why are the soldier so aggressive?"

"Do you see the smoke over there", Vladimir says.Alba nods.

"The soldiers said it's only a fire and everything is under control. I'm sure that's not the truth. Something serious must have happened. It was probably an ambush. There has been a lot of terrorist activity around here."

Alba astonished: "You mean an ambush here? Nearby?" Vladimir calmly answers: "Well, here, we are at war. Things like this can happen at any time."

A huge helicopter thunders by. The driver turns the car around. Alba is shouting over the noise:

"Where are we going?"

"The soldiers have shown him a short-cut to the Military base. Obviously, they don't want us to pass the site where the smoke is rising, Vladimir shouts back.

"Let's hope that he is not driving back to Mozdok!"

The noise of the helicopter dies down.

Soon after the helicopter lands near the destroyed convoy, soldiers are clearing away the damage. A line of body bags are waiting for transport.

26. The Suicide Bomber.

The ad-lib taxi arrives at the Khankala-HQ. The Adjutant General approaches. He greets Vladimir, Alba and Liz and tells Vladimir: "The General is waiting for you. Who are your companions?"

"They're from the UK. They are making a documentary about terrorism." Vladimir turns to Alba and Liz:

"Show him your documents."

Alba and Liz take out their papers and hand them over. The Adjutant General checks them thoroughly and seems satisfied: "Please follow me."

He turns and rushes through the camp. Vladimir, Alba and Liz have difficulties following him. Alba catches up to the Adjutant General:

"Sir, actually I came here to meet some Spetsnaz officers, in particular Captain Sokolov."

The Adjutant General says straight-faced:

"Ah, really? The Captain's mission is already over."

"What do you mean? Is he gone", Alba inquires.

The noise of a helicopter thundering away interrupts them. The Adjutant General looks at the sky, relieved:

"Yes, the Captain is gone."

"But where did he go", Alba asks.

"To Mozdok."

"Sir, I have just come from there", Alba disbelievingly says.

"That's a pity. Well, Miss Smith, what can I do for you now?"

Alba looks at the Adjutant General with a smile:

"Yes, you can do something for me. I have to go back to Mozdok immediately."

"Maybe we can arrange something, Miss Smith. Now I have to leave you, the General is waiting for Comrade Dudkin."

He turns around to Vladimir and orders:

"Follow me!"

Alba sticks to her guns and follows the Adjutant General. On the way to the General's office a picturesque picture presents itself to Alba. Three children are playing in the shadow of a tank while a couple of goats and sheep graze peacefully nearby. Alba remarks to the Adjutant General:

"What an idyllic picture. Or is it a scene about the calm before the storm?"

"It's exactly as you see it", he responds coldly.

Alba turns to Liz: "Please take some shots here."

The Adjutant General stops and puts a good face on a terrible story. Liz gets closer and starts to film the children.

A young soldier jumps from behind the tank. He holds his Kalashnikov very tightly to his body. Alba asks Vladimir:

"Please tell him that we didn't want to disturb him."

Vladimir translates for the young soldier who tells him that it doesn't matter. Alba steps forward and introduces the party to the soldier: "I am Alba from London, this is my friend Liz, also from London and this is Vladimir from Moscow."

Vladimir translates for her. The young soldier smiles:

"My name is Kirill. I am from Novosibirsk."

They shake hands. Vladimir continues to translate. Alba says: "That's quite far away from home. Don't you get homesick?"

Kirill avoids looking at the Adjutant General: "Yes, I do. Especially now that my brother is gone."

Ready to interfere, the Adjutant General steps closer to the group. Alba ignores him:

"Did your brother go back to Novosibirsk?"

The young soldier shakes his head in sadness: "No."

The Adjutant General shouts: "That´s enough!" Alba decisively asks: "Please let me continue!" The Adjutant General stone-facedly orders:

"The General is waiting. You will come with me now."

Alba and Vladimir run beside the Adjutant General. Liz is busy putting her camera back into her shoulder bag and remains a couple of meters behind. While doing so, she observes a boy approaching a unit of about 20 young soldiers who stand in front of a tent talking with the war correspondent Comrade Saizew.

The war correspondent looks at the boy in a very strange way. Somehow he seems to be troubled. Without hesitating Liz takes her camera and starts to film the scene. The Adjutant General stops, turns around and sees Liz filming.

Suddenly, he and Liz are thrown to the ground by an an explosion that rips through the air. The tent blows up, together with the soldiers and the boy. The military base descends into chaos. Inhuman cries come from the dying and injured people lying on the ground. Soldiers are panicking and medics hurry by.

The Adjutant General is the first one to get back on his feet. He rushes toward Liz who lies like dead on the ground with the camera beside her. He grabs for the camera, calls for the medics and leaves the site of the deadly attack.

Vladimir, who seems to be uninjured, helps Alba to get on her feet. Together they hurry to Liz who is already put on a stretcher by the combat medics. Liz gestures to Alba when she is taken away and whispers:

"The Adjutant General has stolen my camera. I have filmed everything. It was a suicide bomber, a boy not older than 9 years..."

Alba gently touches Liz's right hand and nods in agreement.

All three are brought to a tent where the Army Surgical Hospital is lodged and undergo a fast medical check.

It turns out that it was a close shave for all of them. Only Liz is suffering from a couple of cuts and burns on her legs and a medic orders her to stay in the Army Surgical Hospital for observation a couple of hours.

In the meantime, Alba and Vladimir are escorted to a little stone house with barred tiny windows by two soldiers, The house, containing 3 cells, looks like a prison. A rusty iron door of one of the cells is opened with an equally rusty old key.

The two soldiers are quite embarrassed when they order Alba and Vladimir to step into the cell.

The cell is dimly lit by a dirty bulb. The only furniture is an old cot, leaning against the damp wall under the tiny barred window. As soon as the two soldiers are gone Vladimir jumps on the cot and looks through the tiny, barred window. He tries to analyse the situation outside to find a way to escape. While Vladimir is looking out of the window, Alba informs Vladimir saying:

"Liz made me understand that she has everything on film. But the Adjutant General has stolen her camera with the film. We need it back."

Vladimir turns around and looks at Alba:

"Liz will surely get the camera back, but not the film. The Adjutant General will explain that Liz became a witness to an unfortunate incident and that the film is the evidence of how a grenade can explode all by itself."

Alba is irritated: "If he wants to keep it, it's not a problem."

Vladimir jumps down from the cot and turns to Alba:

"The General and his Adjutant are coming to visit us."

The door is unlocked and opens. The General and his Adjutant enter. The Adjutant General holds Alba´s bag and her mobile phone: "Miss Smith, please do excuse us. But this happened for your own security. Please check if there is anything missing."

He hands the bag and the mobile back to Alba. She takes it: "Thank you, Sir, for being so concerned about my security."

Now the General addresses Alba:

"Miss Smith, we are sorry that you became a witness to this unfortunate incident. But maybe your film will help to explain how a grenade could explode all by itself."

The Adjutant General holds up the tape. Alba stares at Vladimir in disbelief. Alba accuses the Adjutant General:

"Sir, you saw what happened!"

He doesn't react. Alba continues: "General, your Adjutant may consider it an accident, but it was an act of terror. A boy, probably no more than 9 years old, blew himself up and killed many of your soldiers!"

The General doesn´t bat an eye: "We understand that you're in a state of shock, and we would like to offer you whatever help and support we can. Unfortunately, I have to inform you that every foreign journalist has to leave Chechnya immediately. Miss Crawford is already on the aircraft which is waiting to bring you out of the emergency zone."

Alba is ready to fight: "No problem. But I won't leave without the tape!"

The Adjutant General informs her: "It will be sent to you as soon as our experts have examined the material. Now, and most importantly, we must take care of your personal safety. The helicopter is waiting."

The door opens. Four armed officers enter. One of them steps in front of the General and announces:

"General, you are under arrest!"

In the confusion that follows, Alba hurls her bag against the stunned Adjutant General and grabs the tape he is still holding.

Vladimir takes Alba's hand and runs out of the cell with her. Nobody is following the two journalists and the helicopter with Liz inside is waiting to take them away.

Part II

The Antidote

27. She brings me luck.

Volgograd railway station. It is the main railway station of the city of Volgograd, Russia, formerly known as Stalingrad, and before that as Tsaritsyn.

The station is one of the largest in Russia and serves long-distance trains and suburban trains, the hub for services to five main destinations: Krasnodar, Rostov-on-Don, Moscow, Saratov and Astrakhan.

The building is an example of the Stalinist architecture style which was popular in Russia from the 1930s until Stalin's death in the 1950s. The building is made of a combination of brick and concrete, the façade consists of ornamental granite.

An old run-down army bus arrives in front of the imposing entrance of the railway station of Volgograd.

Yuri followed by Dmitry and his other men jump out of the army bus with heavy equipment on their backs. The soldiers go directly to the entrance of the railway station and enter the three-story building with a ground floor tower crowned with a spire. The interior walls are mainly marble. The ceiling is decorated with stucco and several paintings of the battles that took place in the city. It's crowded.

Many people of different origins rush to their trains. Yuri and his men get some cigarettes and some snacks at a kiosk. Without hurrying they walk down the platform where their train is waiting. Yuri's mobile phone rings. He takes it out of his pocket and pauses in front of one of the train carriages while his men enter the train. Dmitry remains at a safe distance to Yuri. Yuri says into the mobile: "Yuri Sokolov... Miss Smith! I can hardly hear you." The line goes dead. Yuri informs Dmitry: "It was Alba. We got disconnected."

Dmitry suggests to walk a little further. Maybe the connection will be better over there. Yuri and Dmitry continue to walk down the platform.

Suddenly, fast steps resound behind Yuri and Dmitry.

A group of people who don't look Russian are hurrying toward them. A blond- haired athletic man in his fifties is in their midst. They come closer and Yuri turns slightly. His eyes meet those of the blond-haired man for a fraction of a second. Yuri stops and lets him pass by. Dmitry surprisingly remarks: "You let him pass in front of you. You never did that with anybody before!"

Yuri pensively looks at Dmitry. The mobile rings again. Yuri picks it up and smiles after a moment: "Yes, now I hear you much better." Dmitry grins. Yuri says to Alba:

"We are on our way back to St. Petersburg. No, the mission wasn't successful. I lost the youngest of my men. Now I have to bury him."

Yuri observes how the blond-haired man and his companions stop in front of one of the railway carriages where many people are gathered. Yuri continues his conversation with Alba:

"It's very kind of you to say that, but to protect others is my work. I have to tell you, Khankala is no place to be for a woman. In case you didn't notice, there is a war going on! Do you need any help?"

Meanwhile, the blond-haired man hugs everybody heartily. People hand him little gifts. There are only happy faces around him. Yuri states: "I am glad that you are protected. Vladimir Dudkin is well known and a courageous journalist. I had the pleasure of meeting him some time ago."

A Kalmucken lady steps in front of the blond-haired man. She is holding a long object in her right hand. Yuri, who is still observing the scene, recognises her. It's the brave headmistress of the school in Elista. The blond-haired man takes the headmistress in his strong arms and touches her forehead with his.

Yuri still talks to Alba: "The work you are doing is very important and I am really interested. We will meet in St. Petersburg. There, we will have time to discuss everything, I promise. Thank you. I will tell Dmitry. Be careful. Good-bye."

Yuri smiles at Dmitry: "Best wishes from Liz. You like her, don't you?"

Yuri puts the mobile back into his breast pocket. There, his fingers touch something smooth. He pulls out the object; it's the plastic coated photo of the blond-haired man.

"Yes, I like Liz", Dmitry confirms, "and what about you? Do you like Alba?"

"Yes, I do. She is a very special woman and she is quite beautiful."

For a moment Yuri looks at the photo and then turns in the direction of the blond-haired man saying to Dmitry:

"She brings me luck. Do you remember the Kalmukan lady?"

In this moment the headmistress hands the blond-haired man the long object and says: "Lama, that is a gift from all our friends of our centre in Elista."

Dmitry nods: "Sure I remember her. She is the brave headmistress of the school in Elista and the man over there is the man on the photo. Did the headmistress give this to you?"

Yuri confirms and orders: "Let's move closer. I want to hear what he says."

The Antidote

28. Do you understand that we are really free.

The Lama opens the gift the headmistress gave him. It is a scroll and it appears to be an old Tibetan painting. The Lama addresses himself to the headmistress:

"Vera, thank you very much. It's a very beautiful thangka."

For a moment the Lama concentrates on the thangka, then he holds it up: "This is a simple rendering, but useful."

A blond woman standing next to him looks around critically and remarks: "We need more light. Let's go over there."

The whole group moves under a beautiful lamp from the 40s on the platform. Now the blond-haired man and the blond woman hold the thangka together and show it to the people around them.

"What you see here", the Lama says, "shows the life of beings, and is a representation of their experiences after death."

The Lama points at the Wheel:

"The Wheel of Life shows the six worlds or states of mind and is held by Yama, the Tibetan Lord of Death. The face seen above and the jaw below is not a being, but represent the fact that everything is changing and nothing truly lasts.

Above and to the right as you look at the picture, Buddha points to the moon, which is the way out. It represents the opposite of the Wheel of Life, mind's enlightened and timeless state. It reflects everything but isn't caught by anything anymore.

The Wheel of Life shows the psychological mess beings create in the grip of impermanence, also called the conditioned world. The picture below represents the world of animals, ghosts and states of paranoia. One should do everything to avoid going there."

Now the Lama points at the upper half of the Wheel of Life: "And here there are better, but still not perfect offerings, in the upper half of the wheel. They depict relatively good situations, the lives of gods, half-gods and humans".

Yuri moves closer, so it's easier to see what is going on. Dmitry follows him. Dmitry says to Yuri: "Isn't that the picture that was in the school?"

Yuri nods: "I was wondering what it was all about."

The Lama continues: "Please understand that all the situations represented here are dreams. They're produced by mind but still felt to be real.

It's the same with our human existence, here and now. If we look at the Wheel of Life from the top down, first we see the world of gods of desire. The formless and formed realms above them are difficult to depict.

If the strongest tendency coming up from the subconscious after death is pride, most beings will arrive at the so-called desire god realm, where every wish is immediately fulfilled. Here everything happens that you want and this goes on and on until all the good impressions, which brought one to that state, are used up."

The Lama points to the next scene on the thangka and says: "Sometimes beings' strongest tendency is jealousy. Then the world of demigods appears and their experience of existence is formed by jealousy and some pleasant karma. Because of their good stored impressions they experience having a beautiful and powerful body and things shine, though not as intensely as in the god realms. However the problem is that they are never satisfied. And if they don't fight with the gods, they fight among themselves.

The existence of a half-god is more dangerous than that of a god. Gods only experience dying when their heads are cut off while half-gods feel that they also die when they are stabbed. Therefore the mortality rate among half-gods is higher and if they die with a feeling of anger, their next existence is very unpleasant."

The Lama looks around on the platform and continues to explain: "About human life I will say only a little. You Russians are closely acquainted to its many aspects, both historically and from your rich literature. My Western students mainly know about the rough conditions of life from our excellent press. Basically, we are born, then we try to get what we want and avoid what we don't like, to hold on to what we have and try to manage with what we cannot avoid. Then old age, sickness and death follow. Human life has a special quality, however. It holds the possibility for conscious interaction, enlightenment and the ability to benefit countless beings."

The Lama pauses and looks at the people who are gathering around him before he continues:

"Do we have an old text about the Wheel of Life? It's interesting to see how much the world has changed."

Vera steps forward and says: "Yes, I've got one. It's from my grandmother."

Vera hands it to the Lama: "Vera, would you like to read it for us?"

Vera smiles: "Very much."

The Lama continues to explain: "It's written in a language from the Middle Ages so I will add some commentaries later."

Now Vera is reading formally: "The animals that live in the realm of gods and humans suffer continually from their stupidity and from being exploited, while the Nagas pass their lives in misery being tormented by Garudas and rains of burning sand. In addition they are stupid, aggressive and poisonous. The wild animals that share our human world, in particular, live in constant fear. They cannot eat a single mouthful of food without being on their guard. They have many mortal enemies, for all animals prey on each other and there are always hunters".

Now the Lama is adding a comment to the old the text Vera just read: "It's also possible that confusion is the strongest tendency in the mind. If we have consciously led other people astray or relied on lies too often, rather than using our human potential, we may experience an animal rebirth. The mind of the dead one will try to hide between rocks, bushes or in other places where animals come to mate and will go between them. Hopefully, if one is lucky, this state will only last for one life-time".

The Lama points to the next scene on the Wheel of Life and says:

"Some people have greed as their main tendency. If this is the case, they may experience deep and massive frustration."

Vera turns the loose pages of the Tibetan-style book and continues to read formally:

"Pretas are tormented by extreme hunger and thirst. Centuries pass by and they never even hear the word water, let alone have some to drink. They are constantly obsessed with food and drink, searching for them endlessly, and never finding the smallest trace. From time to time, far away, they catch sight of a stream of clear, pure water. But their joints are too fragile to take the weight of their bellies, so they can't reach it."

The Lama goes on with the comment:

"Like the other two lower and painful worlds, you see them clearest in mental institutions. The experience is much stronger, however, when mind is not distracted by the sensory experiences of having a body. Here you see the ghosts. Among ghosts, all desires and wishes focus on eating and drinking, but one finds no satisfaction. In the drawing you see how outer and inner factors come together. What these beings try to eat becomes fire and they can hardly move their enormous bodies with their thin limbs. Greed is surely not something noble!"

The Lama points at the Wheel of Life once more and says:

"Lastly the worst of all psychological states. Here, even scientific terms fail. Let us hear the ancient text, Vera."

Vera again reads formally:

"In the hells one experiences only suffering. A human tortured without break with 300 different torture instruments at the same time, wouldn't come close to a fraction of the suffering beings experience in these realms. They are tortured, again and again, until the situation turns around and the victims become the perpetrators, and the perpetrators the victims."

The Lama also comments on this worst of all psychological states:

"In today's psychological climate we might explain these worlds like this: If hate and anger are the strongest tendency after death, we will experience real paranoia. At that time, because we receive no new impressions, all mind's negative imprints will surface and these tendencies will lead to dramatic suffering. Buddha describes 18 extremely painful states of paranoia, which it is possible to fall into and again you only need to visit a mental hospital to see what a suffering mind may bring upon itself."

Here the Lama pauses for a moment before he continues:

"So, back to us humans. The painting is too compelling to simply pass by. We appear in these bodies when desire is the strongest feeling in our mind. After death, when our mind is in the state of awareness and energy, we will look for our future parents. We will be attracted when they are making love and enter at the crown of the father's head or through his mouth. Then we follow the sperm to the womb of the mother and remain there as an energy-field until the semen and egg unite. The next seven weeks are spent in an unconscious state like deep sleep. Then, as the embryo develops ever more, we gradually remember scenes from our last life. The end of pregnancy and birth itself are experienced as very painful. The texts say that we feel like being squeezed out between metal plates. And then the wheel of conditioned existence turns once more".

Now the thangka is passed around and Yuri also gets to look at it. He raises his eyes and meets the eyes of the Lama. The Lama is talking directly to Yuri now:

"In the middle of the thangka are the three causes of the whole mix up: Basic confusion is represented by a pig, attachment by a rooster and aversion by a snake. When those three factors are active, the events depicted here become unavoidable. These states are called Samsara or the Wheel of Life and they are a sticky affair. It is most difficult to get out of such situations. Not being aware of cause and effect, one is caught in them. One is constantly driven from one confused state to another and therefore alternates between the six trips that were just described. However mixed-up beings' outer and inner worlds may appear, moreover, the experience is always timeless radiant space and also won't disappear or change. This is what Buddha wants us to know and which will liberate and enlighten whoever recognizes it. Things appear in mind, are known by it, play around there and dissolve there again. Both outwardly as the world we perceive, and inwardly, like our thoughts and feelings, it is only a dream. What we have to remove is the basic ignorance that they are real and that they exist by themselves."

The Lama takes the thangka and pretends to tap it on the head of a young woman. He laughs and says to the young woman: "Don't take more blessings from the conditioned world. You have enough of those and they don't do us much good."

He looks around his students and continues joyfully:

"Did you understand that we are really free? That we can trust space and the moment? Both gods and devils, as well as pleasant and painful events are created by mind and one receives whatever one puts into the world. Heaven and hell happens between our own ears, ribs or wherever we think our mind is. To reach that insight, however, the old rules still apply. There is a great difference between feeding one's consciousness with good or bad impressions. From the good mental states you can wake up into liberation and enlightenment, whereas the bad ones only bring more difficulties. Even at the most pleasant times, don't stop noticing how Samsara, the conditioned world, is a marketplace where everybody looks for illusory happiness. Only mind's essence, however, is lasting and perfect happiness, and that occurs naturally when mind recognizes itself."

At this point everybody had a look at the thangka including Yuri and Dmitry. The thangka is given back to the Lama. He rolls it carefully together and hands it to the blond women next to him. With gratitude and a smile he turns to Vera: "Thank you for travelling all the way with us to Volgograd. In the winter I'll teach at your center in Elista."

The time has come for the Lama to take leave of all his students and friends who are not travelling on with him. He hugs them warmly or he touches their foreheads with his metal box, a Gau, before he gets on the train.

Yuri and Dmitry board the train through a different door. Shortly after, the doors close and the train starts to move. One last time, the Lama leans out of the train window:

"There's one more thing you should tell all friends. Yama isn't meant to be put in the meditation room where the enlightened forms are. It should be placed at the entry to the meditation room, because it shows us what we cannot rely upon. It is foolish to trust the conditioned world. The pictures should make us practice even harder. As our western centres are growing so well, I will now try to spend two months in Russia every year. See you again soon."

The Antidote

29. For the sake of everyone, try to avoid feeling angry!

The train is heading towards towards Moscow. The Lama sits in a window-seat and writes on a manuscript. Rebecca, the blond woman, and a man are busily working on their laptops. From time to time, the people who are travelling with the Lama appear to ask questions or to be touched with the Gau from around his neck. Somehow they don't want to leave and Rebecca must ask them to give the Lama peace and quiet to work. That goes on until late evening.

Now it is quiet on the train. Most of the passengers are asleep. Rebecca collects the papers which the Lama was working on and while preparing the compartment for sleeping she says to the Lama: "It's 4 o'clock again. We need to get some sleep."

The Lama puts away his manuscript and gets up. He hugs Rebecca and gives her a kiss saying:

"Isn't it exciting? We are actually growing. Even in this busy world we are keeping Buddha's highest teachings alive. The Diamond Way is growing. A billion communist Chinese got hit with a lot of egg in their faces. Though they hoped to have destroyed our transmission together with Tibet, it made us modern and strong."

The Lama steps out of the compartment, stretches for a moment and opens the old wooden stuck window with a strong jerk. He looks into the clear night.

A man approaches silently. It is Yuri. He stops by the side of the Lama and both men look into the clear night.

The Lama addresses Yuri: "What a beautiful night. There's a full moon."

Yuri points to the moon and says: "It's the way out", you explained, "and it represents the opposite, the mind's enlightened and timeless state. It reflects everything but isn't caught by anything anymore. I can repeat what you said but I don't think I understand it. Two days ago I sent one of my men to his death. It's the first time that one of my men died."

"What was his name", the Lama asks.

"Sergey. He was only 27 years old. I saw him die and he was afraid."

The Lama looks at Yuri: "Yes, he and countless others. Our lives come and go, however, and for a wise man there is no need to be afraid of death. Bodies die, but mind cannot. It is always timeless space. That awareness, which looks through our eyes right now, is not a thing and therefore it can't be destroyed. In essence it is space, so it can't die. You may have guessed that I'm a Buddhist teacher, a Lama. We actually have methods that give one control through and beyond death. Among them are certain vibrations, called mantras. If they are used with a compassionate motivation, they bring mind where we wish it to go."

Yuri cuts the Lama off with a quick laugh:

"Lama, if I get sentimental, even for a split second, either my men or I will die."

"I'm not talking about fuzziness or sentimentality here. Compassion becomes activity, it brings us beyond our problems. It produces lasting and very powerful kinds of activity. This feeling activates everything in you. Including your fighting skills and awareness of possible dangers! Your protective feelings towards your men show that its force is actually driving you already!"

Yuri hands the coated photo to him and says: "That's you, isn't it?"

The Lama looks at it and confirms: "Yes, it's me."

"It was given to me by the lady who gave you the thangka, after my men and I rescued the children who were taken as hostages in her school."

The Lama answers still holding the coated photo:

"Yes, I know, Vera told me. You choose to risk your lives to create a more human world. You protect children, women and the weak."

"I am not at all sure about the happiness I'm creating. When we pick up our Kalashnikovs, it's already hell", Yuri remarks.

The Lama blows on the photo, gives it back to Yuri and says:

"Your effectiveness and survival depend on your distance to your feelings. If you don't dissolve even the finest veils of anger or frustration into space, you will not see clearly. Instead, you'll make the same mistakes as your fanatic enemy. The longer you are under fire and the more you see your friends die, the more easily it can happen. Please be very careful now."

The Lama is getting philosophical hoping that the soldier will understand and continues:

"Maybe these Buddhist points will remove some edges and sharp points from your life. In Buddhism we think that the brain does not produce, but instead transforms mind. That it is the receiver and not the sender of the stream of experiences that beings think they are and identify with. I have some memories of protecting Eastern Tibetans civilians against Chinese soldiers in my last life. I've travelled secretly in Tibet and have recognized several of those places, which we have also confirmed. You may say I'm more a program than a man, more motivated by what I have promised to do than by any wishes of my own. I think we may have fought together at that time and this is why we are meeting now. While in this life you again protect peoples' bodies and outer freedoms, it has become my job to protect their inner freedom and minds. You work more with the effects and I with the causes. May we both have much success!"

The Lama pauses for a moment before he continues:

"Shoot at the legs if you can and if killing is necessary, feel like a doctor who inflicts a smaller pain on one being in order to avoid a larger one for many later. The free world needs people like you. But, for the sake of everyone, try to avoid feeling angry."

Yuri takes his watch from his wrist, hands it to the Lama and says: "Thank you, Lama."

Yuri turns around and is about to leave. The Lama quickly takes off his black American Air force jacket and says:

"Warrior!"

Yuri turns back. The Lama hands him the jacket and a piece of paper that turns out to be his travel plan:

"I will focus on Sergey. He will meet with the Buddha of Limitless Light now. There is nothing you can do which will bring him back. Come and see me in Moscow if you can. I will teach you Phowa, a Tibetan method for entering a state of highest bliss at death. It will change your life. I give a dozen five-day courses in Europe, Russia and in Siberia each year."

The Lama takes the Gau, from around his neck. He puts one hand behind Yuri's neck and pulls him towards himself. He presses the Gau to Yuri's head, then to his throat and at last to his heart. After standing quietly together for some time, the Lama releases Yuri, smiles at him, turns and walks away.

30. A first class ticket for the way out.

Volkovo Cemetery is one of the largest and oldest non-Orthodox cemeteries in Saint Petersburg, Russia. Until the early 20th century it was one of the main burial grounds for Lutheran Germans in Russia. It is estimated that over 100,000 people have been buried at this cemetery since 1773.

It is raining heavily. Yuri is standing in front of Sergey's coffin. He's wearing the black leather jacket the Lama gave him and holds an umbrella over Sergey's mother. Her eyes are red and swollen.

Dmitry, Mikhail, Andrey, Sasha, Kirill and the other men of Yuri's unit stand behind them. Yuri says some words in front of the coffin.

Sergey's mother takes Yuri's hand and squeezes it as a sign of gratitude. Then she takes a step towards the coffin and bends her head. For some time she remains motionless. When she steps back, Yuri does the same and speaks to the dead Sergey in a low voice:

"Everything is arranged my friend. The photo of the blond-haired man I pressed to your heart when you were dying is a Lama, a Buddhist teacher and a Master of a method called Phowa. He teaches Phowa and learning it is just like winning a first class ticket for the way out of this mess. He promised he will take care of you."

Raising his head, Yuri notices a figure under a tree holding an umbrella and a large bunch of white roses. It is Alba. For a moment they look at each other.

Yuri steps back and all the others, Sergey's friends and relatives say goodbye to Sergey, each of them in their own way.

31. Money attracts most people.

Yuri, his entire unit and Alba gather in the small apartment where Sergey was living with his mother. Sergey's mother serves food. Alba offers her help. She refuses and encourages Alba to enjoy the company of the other guests.

Mikhail reaches for Sergey's guitar and starts to play Strawberry fields forever. Alba sits next to Yuri and says:

"That's such a wonderful song."

Mikhail turns to Alba and asks: "Do you know the words?" Alba reflects for a moment before saying: "I will try to remember them. My dad always played this song when he returned from Vietnam."

Alba concentrates and starts singing the Beatles' song:

"Let me take you down, cause I'm going to Strawberry Fields. Nothing is real, and nothing to get hung about. Fields forever. Living is easy with eyes closed, misunderstanding all you see. It's getting hard to be some-one but it all works out, it doesn't matter much to me. Let me take you down, cause I'm going to Strawberry Fields. Nothing is real and nothing to get hung about. Strawberry Fields forever. No one I think is in my tree, I mean it must be high or low. That is you can't you know tune in but it's all right, that is I think it's not too bad. Let me take you down, cause I'm going to Strawberry Fields. Nothing is real, and nothing to get hung about. Strawberry Fields forever. I think I know I mean a "Yes" but it's all wrong, that is I think I disagree. Let me take you down, cause I'm going to Strawberry Fields. Nothing is real, and nothing to get hung about. Strawberry Fields forever. Strawberry Fields forever."

After the last notes of the song, there's silence. Then all the men clap their hands. Sergey's mother says with tears in her eyes: "Alba, thank you very much. You have such a beautiful voice. Mikhail played this wonderful song on Sergey's 27th birthday. That was just three weeks ago."

She starts crying heartbreakingly. Alba takes her in her arms and holds her tightly until she calms down, gets up and goes back to the kitchen.

Alba addresses the men with tears in her eyes:

"This war is insane. It's taking the lives of so many young men. Even children throw bombs, killing others and themselves."

Her statement is met with silence. Alba wipes her tears away and continues:

"It was Ali Moussa and his henchmen. Wasn't it? They killed Sergey."

Yuri answers coldly: "Yes." Alba looks at him: "I really don't understand why a criminal like Ali Moussa can still strike terror into people's hearts! I mean, couldn't you catch him?"

"Yes, we could. But we have to get the order to be able to act."

"It might be a good idea to put a reward on his head. Money attracts most people", Alba advices.

Yuri's eyes and voice go ice-cold: "I would kill him without being rewarded, and all of my men would do the same. It's a matter of honour." All of Yuri's men nod in agreement.

"You would kill him", Alba astonished asks.

"Yes, and before he died, I would make him understand what he has done to all the people he has killed", responds Yuri with a bitter expression in his face.

"What? You mean you could actually torture someone?"

"If it helps to protect others, yes".

Alba is appalled and looks at Sergey's mother who just steps into the room and nods sadly.

Yuri looks at Alba and says now with a calm voice:

"Well, I could also arrest him and hand him to the authorities. Then he could be tried in public and they would probably lock him up, in the psychiatric prison. Is this how I should handle the patient?"

Alba´s face brightens up: "Would you do that?"

"For you I would do this and more."

32. Win or die.

The wake is over. Dmitry is at the steering wheel of his old Russian car. He drives through the streets of St. Petersburg very fast. Yuri sits next to him, Alba is in the back seat finishing a conversation on her mobile with Liz. Alba informs Yuri that they would like to show him the material about the young suicide bomber she filmed in Khankala. He agrees.

Due to Dmitry's sporty driving style, they arrive shortly afterwards at the Hotel where Alba and Liz are staying. It is located in the heart of St. Petersburg next to St. Isaac's Cathedral and close to one of the most important museums of the world, the Hermitage. Dmitry leaves his car in front of the Hotel.

The doorman of the Hotel is not very pleased to look after such an old car, since he is used to luxurious cars and to big tips.

The three cross the beautiful entertainment hall of the Hotel and enter the elevator which brings them to the 3rd floor. Nobody talks. All three are absorbed in their thoughts.

The elevator door opens and Liz stands in front of it. Liz is all smiles when she sees Dmitry. First she greets Yuri and then she embraces Dmitry. Alba looks at her slightly surprised. Liz looks different. She has put on some make-up and is wearing a short skirt and a tight t-shirt. Alba has never seen Liz in a skirt or a dress. Alba chuckles.

Liz asks the two men to follow her in her room. The two men enter an elegantly furnished Hotel room and sit down on the stylish armchairs. She offers coffee and the men accept gratefully. Liz starts the video. Silently they watch the film to the end.

Afterwards Yuri looks at the two young women and says:

"You have risked your lives. It was very brave of you to go to such a place. Now you would like to do the promised interview, I suppose."

Alba happily answers: "Yes, that would be great."

"Okay, let's start working."

Liz gets her camera ready. Alba excuses herself and disappears in the bathroom.

Yuri informs Liz: "The deputy Commander can't be filmed." Liz nods and smiles at Dmitry: "That's for security reasons. Yes, Captain, I understand."

Alba comes back from the bathroom. Yuri turns around. Alba looks beautiful. She has put on some make up and pinned up her hair.

Alba sits on the sofa opposite Yuri. He lights a cigarette and signals Alba that he is ready for her to begin. Alba starts off the interview:

"Captain, you are a commander of a Spetsnaz unit, a special task force, known as one of the most formidable units in the world."

"Like the British SAS, the US Navy Seals, the Delta-Force,the French 2nd REP, the German KSK and the Sajeret Matkal from Israel", Yuri answers.

"You are specialized in anti-terrorism and are a hostage-rescue expert", Alba goes on questioning, "You are responsible for hunting down terrorists and liberating hostages all over Russia. In your line of work your life is continually in danger. You could be wounded, tortured, taken prisoner or even killed. Are you ever afraid?"

"No", Yuri answers and continues," if a Spetsnaz soldier was afraid he wouldn't be able to do this job. There are criteria for joining the

Spetsnaz. First we go through various arduous physical and psychological tests. If we pass these we undergo a special training program which
has been developed to improve such qualities as fearlessness."

"Can you tell us more about it", Alba inquires.

"One can develop fearlessness through training. We learn Karate and
other martial-art techniques to protect others and ourselves. We study
Coding so that we are able to influence people by using particular gestures and colours amongst other things. In addition, we learn hypnosis
and train our mind with meditation."

"If I understood correctly," Alba says, "your work is focused on protecting people. What about when you need to kill others?"

"Well, we also learn 121 ways to kill", Yuri reflects for a moment before
he says:

"One can be a soldier and protect people but one should not be
angry with the enemy or enjoy it when pulling the trigger."

"Well said!"

Alba is impressed by Yuri's knowledge and understanding and continues to inquire:

"How is it possible not be angry with the enemy who for example
killed women, children, soldiers and even tortured them?"

"One of my teachers told me that our effectiveness and survival depend
on our distance to our feelings. If we don't dissolve even the finest veils of
anger or frustration into space, we will not see clearly. Instead, we'll make
the same mistakes as our fanatic enemy. The longer we are under fire and
the more we see our friends die, the easier it is that we may get angry."

"Please could you give me the name of your teacher please", Alba
smiles, "I could use some of his advice as well. I have many questions
about life and the meaning of life."

"I'm sorry, but that's not possible. This is secret information." Yuri
smiles. Alba winks: "I understand", and gets back to the topic:

"How would you define Spetsnaz?"

Yuri says without any hesitation:

"Win or die."

Alba looks at Yuri: "Could one say that up to now, you have always won?" Yuri grins: "As you can see, I am alive and in very good health." Alba gets serious again:

"How long have you been doing this job?"

"My first mission was in Afghanistan in 1979. That was 22 years ago. Now I am 41 years old."

"What was your task during the Afghanistan war?"

"At that time Mustafa ben Ammar first started funding military camps to train men to fight against the Russian army. That happened with the support of the American government", Yuri explains.

"We have been hearing his name more and more frequently recently", Alba says, but there is little hard evidence about his activities. Does he really exist?"

"Yes, he does. He is a rich Saudi or Yemenite and a terrorist and a jihadist on an international level. He finances terrorism in many countries around the world. Now, he is hiding in Afghanistan, under the protection of the Government."

"Does Ali Moussa, who plays a leading role as a terrorist in the Chechen war, belong to his group?"

"He and many others were already active during the Afghan war. This Holy War has been the basis for international terrorism today", Yuri explains, "Moussa was one of ben Ammar's favourite and most talented pupils. He belongs to his network. There is evidence of substantial financial support for Moussa from ben Ammar. He is also known as "The Godfather of Terrorism" for his generous donations to the cause".

Yuri's pager beeps. He immediately stands. Liz stops filming and says: "There is a phone in the bedroom. Please help yourself." Yuri disappears in the bedroom. Alba watches him as he leaves the room. Alba worriedly asks Dmitry: "Do you have to go?"

"The commander will tell us ", Dmitry answers.

Yuri steps back into the room and says looking at Alba:

"I am sorry, duty calls. We have to leave."

Alba disappointedly hands Yuri a video: "Here's a copy for you. Is there a possibility to finish the interview and get a copy of Moussa's video?"

"I told you already. The work you are doing is very important and I want it to get done. So, of course we'll finish the interview."

Yuri takes the mobile out of his pocket and hands it to Alba: "Before I forget, I think this is yours."

Alba refuses to take the phone: "Give it back to me when our work is finished. Okay?"

"Sure. Actually, it's a luxury for me. Thank you," Yuri replies. The mobile disappears again in one of Yuri's pockets: "Let's stay in touch."

He kisses Alba on the cheek and leaves with Dmitry.

33. In those days he was a remarkable soldier.

Spetsnaz HQ in Saint Petersburg. Yuri and Dmitry enter a building which needs at least paint-work. Only one dim light bulb illuminates Yuri's and Dmitry's way to the office of the Spetsnaz commander through a long and dark corridor.

Yuri knocks on the door. A strong voice answers:

"Captain, come in."

Yuri and Dmitry enter and salute the Spetsnaz commander. He is a tall man who needs more sleep.

He sits at his desk and studies some papers. It's dark in his office apart from an old panel sheet light on his desk. The Spetsnaz Commander is looking at Yuri and Dmitry:

"Good to see you!"

"General, you're up late", Yuri states.

"Captain, I can sleep when the war is over."

Yuri laughs briefly. It's an old joke, an old ritual.

"It's embarrassing, what I hear of General Korsakov", the Commander says," we fought in Afghanistan together. In those days he was a remarkable soldier, an example of courage and honesty. This war is getting more and more out of our hands. Now, finally, Moscow agreed to get rid of the main stumbling block in the war, Ali Moussa. The latest information we have is that he wants to leave Russia. Our intelligence sources said that the Pankisi Gorge is a vital corridor for Chechen rebel fighters and foreign Islamists infiltrating Chechnya to fight us. Now Washington seems to come to the same conclusion. We were also informed that Washington wanted to train counter-terrorist forces in Georgia to tackle the problem."

"The Pankisi Gorge is an extremely dangerous place. There is a rumour that our target will try to escape to Georgia", Yuri informs the Commander.

The Spetsnaz Commander rises and walks to a chart on the wall. Yuri follows him. The Commander says:

"Ali Moussa is wounded." Yuri nods.

The Commander continues:

"I'm sorry about Sergey, he was very courageous. "

Yuri with a sad look in his eyes: "Yes, he was. I should have been more aware of the danger, though."

"I don't want you to make a personal thing out of it!" The Spetsnaz Commander looks at Yuri for a moment and points out three spots on the chart on the wall:

"We know he has three hideouts. Commit these places to memory. Captain, here's your new order: You and your unit are responsible for catching Moussa alive and handing him over to the proper authorities."

Yuri salutes: "Yes, Sir!"

The Commander looks at Dmitry: "Ali Moussa must face a public trial. The world must see that we can handle terrorism."

34. Where are the Protectors?

Alba is about to go to sleep. Dressed in a silk kimono, she stands in front of the mirror in the bathroom of the Hotel. She brushes her hair and talks into her mobile: "Cynthia yes, we have it all on tape. Just 2 feet closer Liz would have been dead. Yes, they tried to suppress it. The General was arrested. The film is not complete yet, I still need the comment from Captain Sokolov and a video to complete the trailer."

The hotel phone rings. Alba is nervously looking at the ringing phone: "Give me, say, forty-eight hours. I've got to go. Bye, Cynthia."

Alba disconnects and picks up the hotel phone:

"Yes? Captain Sokolov! No, no, it is not too late. Please do come up."

Alba puts down the receiver, grabs her clothes, runs into the bathroom and throws them on a chair. Her hand trembles. She puts on some lipstick but smears it. Irritated, she wipes it off, reaches for the perfume bottle and opens it. It slips from her hand, falls on her clothes on the chair and perfume spreads all over.

There is a knock at the door. Alba desperately looks at her clothes, takes a deep breath and walks to the door to open it: "Hi."

"May I come in", Yuri asks.

"Of course!" Alba looks down at herself:

"I need a couple of minutes. I have to get dressed. Oh, and I'll order us some espresso."

Yuri laughs: "You look beautiful. The kimono fits you very well."

Yuri steps in carrying a bottle of champagne, a huge bag of crisps and the video and hands the video to Alba. She calms down and smiles:

"The video. That was fast. Thank you."

Only now Alba notices the bottle of champagne and the huge bag of crisps Yuri still holds in his hands. Alba surprised: "Wow, crisps and champagne! Most people think that this is an odd combination but I love it."

"Odd? Not at all. Besides, it's hard to find good caviar at midnight."

Alba takes two crystal glasses from a silver plate while Yuri opens the bottle and pours the champagne into the glasses. Alba hands one of the glasses to Yuri. She smiles at him. They clink their glasses:

"Shall we drink to your next successful mission?"

Alba asks looking into Yuri's eyes.

"Or to the successful start to your series A World of Terror?", Yuri responds.

"Well, I am thinking of calling it Where are the Protectors? What do you think about the title?"

Gently Yuri takes Alba in his arms: "I am already here!"

Alba can feel Yuri's strong body. First, they don't move. They only enjoy the strong and exciting feeling of their bodies. Then, looking into each other's eyes, they kiss. Alba's kimono opens. Yuri's hand glides over Alba's body. Alba reaches for Yuri's belt and opens it. Yuri wordlessly picks her up and takes her to bed.

35. I can train and protect people's bodies until they die.

The sun is rising. The awakening St Petersburg reveals its full beauty and elegance in an infinite range of golden colours.

Alba wakes up and smiles happily. She reaches for Yuri at the other side of the big bed. He is not there anymore. Alba hears a noise in the bathroom. She smiles and sits up. Yuri walks into the bedroom already dressed. He jumps on the bed, takes Alba in his arms and kisses her.

"You're leaving already", Alba asks.

"Yes. Dmitry is picking me up in ten minutes."

"But it's still so early!"

"We need to get ready. We're leaving for our next assignment soon."

"Are you going abroad?"

"Yes."

Yuri pauses for a moment before saying: "I will be back soon. Hopefully."

"What do you mean or what are you trying to say? Is your mission more dangerous than usual", Alba worriedly inquires.

"It is a mission like any other mission". Yuri smiles.

"I would like to invite you to a special course when I get back, in Moscow." Alba is instantly interested:

"A Protector Course?"

Yuri amused: "Not exactly. Actually it's much more than that. It's a course that goes beyond protection of bodies."

"Will you be the course instructor?"

"No. I can train and protect people's bodies until they die, that's it."

Yuri digs into his breast pocket for the photo of the Lama and hands it to Alba.:

"He is the Master of this course." Alba looks at the photo for some time:

"Wow. What a man! Who is he?"

"He is a Lama, a Buddhist teacher", Yuri explains.

"I heard about Lamas. As far as I understand, it is a title given in Tibetan Buddhism to a venerated spiritual master who embodies the Buddha's teachings!" Yuri nods.

Alba continues with interest: "If you can train and protect people's bodies until they die, then I suppose this Master is going beyond what you can do."

She pauses and looks at Yuri questioningly. Yuri smiles:

"You are quite fast in understanding the big picture. Yes, indeed he is a Master of a Tibetan method called Phowa. He's offering me the chance to learn it, after I told him about the death of Sergey, and that my youngest man was very afraid of dying." Yuri pauses a moment reflecting before he continues with a smile on his face:

"If I understood well, Phowa is a method for entering a state of highest bliss at death and it will change people's lives."

"Phowa. Yes, it sounds very exciting. I would like to learn it very much. Since I was little I wished to learn to meditate. I very often sat down in meditation position under an old pine in the park of my grandmother's villa outside Florence. But...", Alba pauses.

Cynthia wants you to return to London", Yuri responds and continues:

"What about an exclusive interview with an old client of mine? He is in a safe place, a prison called Lefortovo in Moscow."

"You mean, I should interview a terrorist?"

"Yes, I think so. You should do as much research as possible on the subject. Would that be a good enough reason for your boss to let you stay in Russia a little longer? The course we've been talking about will take place in ten days".

Alba exclaims with a radiant smile on her face:

"That means that you are back in ten days!"

Yuri does not respond. There's a knock at the door. Alba looks at door: "That's Dmitry?" Yuri nods.

Alba reaches for Yuri and puts her arms around his neck:

"Thanks. Be careful and be back for the Phowa course, my love."

Alba kisses Yuri first tenderly and then passionately.

36. You should have given him the mask.

Moscow. Alba and Liz arrive early in the morning in a limousine with a private driver at the Moscow state prison, Lefortovo, Energeticheskaya Street.

It is a long way from Moscow's famous tourist attractions, although the area that surrounds it is very interesting historically. The prison is just a few steps from Lefortovo Park, which was named after Franz Lefort, a close associate of Tsar Peter the Great, Russia's great modernizer. Designed to please Peter the Great, it was the very first park in whole Russia. The house of Anna Mons, the Tsar's famous Dutch mistress is just around the corner.

Despite these historical surroundings, Energeticheskaya looks like a typical suburban Moscow street, with its standard-built Stalin-era houses and the prison is difficult to find. It is hidden behind the gloomy and trivial apartment blocks. While all of Moscow's main prisons are described by historians or experts, – even including the internal jail in the FSB's Lubyanka – this is not the case with Lefortovo. Even its design is a mystery: Nobody knows exactly why architect Kozlov in 1881 chose to design this military prison in the form of the letter "K" – with the four house-blocks connected in the center. Some speculated it might be in the honour of Catherine II the Great, Empress of Russia. Somehow, the prison always had close ties with the regime. It soon came to be used as a favourite jail for the regime's political enemies, by Soviet rulers as well as their successors.

The office of the warden of the Lefortovo prison is a meagre and damp place. Two stocky jailers with side weapons in holsters stand at the door and greet the two women as they enter. The warden sits behind a desk of old communist times. He looks very tired and does not stand up to welcome the two women, though he greets them politely.

He opens the drawer of his desk immediately, takes two white face masks from it and hands them to Alba and Liz:

"You'd better use these. We have a tuberculosis problem here and I wouldn't want you to get infected. Use them for your own protection."

The warden stands up behind his desk: "I will bring you to the interrogation room. Please do follow me."

"Can we see where the criminal is held", Alba asks.

"As I told you before, we have a tuberculosis problem here", the warden answers.

Alba and Liz put the masks on. The prison warden thinks for a moment and says:

"Well, Miss Smith, since you have been recommended by Captain Sokolov, I will make an exception for you."

The warden gives a sign to the two stocky jailers to escort the two women on their way to the terrorist's cell. Liz takes out her camera. The warden fiercely snaps:

"You cannot film in the prisoner's cell block!"

Liz pauses, alarmed by his grimness.

The two women are led through a series of dark, narrow, cold and damp passages until they come to an old rusty iron door. One of the jailers looks through a small hole in the rusty door, which is secured with iron bars and shouts:

"Ahmed! Visitors!"

He unlocks the door. Alba and Liz see ten prisoners who sit and stand in the small and dirty cell. There are only four cots made from wooden planks and a bucket instead of a toilet. One prisoner laughs: "Hey, Ahmed, it's your great day!" A second one remarks sarcastically: "Two faithless, impure women are waiting for you."

The warden addresses Alba: "It's a bit overcrowded at the moment."

The dark bearded Ahmed comes forward, holding a book in his hands. On his face are dirt and dried bloodstains and his teeth are black. The jailer handcuffs him and pushes him forward. Ahmed completely ignores Alba and Liz.

In the interrogation room there are two chairs and a table between them. The two stocky jailers stand beside Ahmed, one to his right and one to his left. A third jailer with a truncheon stands at the door.

The warden excuses himself and leaves. Liz sets up her camera and points it directly at Ahmed. She and Alba are wearing their masks.

Ahmed says to Alba: "It's very good that you respect our God's commandments..." he points at the book in front of him, "...and that you are covering your face."

"Your English is very good. Where did you learn it", Alba asks. Ahmed ignores Alba's question and states:

"The Holy Book says that there is no greater affliction to men than women. We are allowed to interrupt our prayer when a black dog, a woman or a donkey passes by."

Liz gives Alba a look of disbelief.

"In our world, a dog is a good friend of mankind. A black one is even considered to be a protector. You really must dislike women to treat them so badly. What about your mother? Do also you treat her this way", Alba asks.

Ahmed responds with cold eyes:

"Women are the cause of all evil of the world. The Holy Book also says that women are inferior to men and that their husbands have the right to scourge them if they are found to be disobedient. It teaches us that women will go to hell if they are disobedient to their husbands."

Alba continues to inquire:

"Is that why the prison guards in fundamentalist regimes rape women they think are apostates before they kill them? Because they believe a virgin cannot go to hell?"

Ahmed does not react and keeps looking at his Holy Book. Alba changes the question:

"You were imprisoned because you engaged in terrorist activities against Russia, and for raping and killing women and children."

Ahmed answers with cold fury: "Our God tells us to kill whoever rejects our religion:

"Kill them until there is no persecution and the only religion is God's", he recites.

Proudly he continues: "Those who disbelieve in our religion are filthy, untouchable and impure. We are ordered to fight the non-believers until no other religion except our true religion is left. The Holy Book says that the non-believers will go to hell and will drink boiling water".

He pauses a moment and continues even more fanatically than before:

"There is only one law that exists, and that is God's word. We have been ordered by him to fight the non-believers until they say "no one has the right to be worshipped but him. The best thing we can do, after believing in God, is to participate in Holy War, in God's cause. Everyone who participates in a Holy War, when not compelled to do so except by belief in God, will be rewarded by him either here or be admitted to paradise if he is martyred", Ahmed drones on.

"So, in the name of your God, you try to eradicate all human beings who don't believe in your God from this world. Hitler, Stalin and Mao have already tried to do something similar. That means more violence, more killing, more terror and unending suffering for mankind", Alba says. Ahmed continues to respond aggressively:

"No. Not suffering. That means the world is being purged." He starts coughing. He is in pain. Alba waits with her next question until he stops coughing. Then she asks: "When do you envision the end to your so-called "purge?" Ahmed answers triumphantly:

"When the world is ruled by holy men, and everyone bows down to God."

Alba's mobile rings. She grabs it and sees that it is Yuri. She excuses herself for a moment, stands up and moves to the other side of the inter-rogation room and takes the mask off quickly. With the most radiant smile she answers the phone:

"Yuri, what a joy to hear you! Are you back? Oh, but you will be back in time for the course, won't you?"

Ahmed jumps up from his chair and shouts hatefully:

"Make the American whore cover her face!"

While talking with Yuri Alba sees how one of the jailers strikes Ahmed with a truncheon. He groans and sinks down to his chair.

Alba says to Yuri: "Yes, I am in the middle of the interview. No, there is no way to reach him. He lives in a world of hate and anger. That is how it is."

Simultaneously Liz nervously takes out her cigarettes and hands the whole packet to the jailers: "Let's take a short break. Please, finish them off. I really should stop smoking. A woman shouldn't smell like an ashtray." The jailers grin. Everybody but Ahmed takes a cigarette. For a moment his eyes narrow and he presses his lips together. Alba looks in his direction. He is bleeding from his head. Liz hands one of the jailers a tissue to give to Ahmed. Alba concentrates on Yuri again:

"Of course, I will call the Lama and arrange everything for a meeting with him. Would you like to meet him before or after the lecture? Okay, no problem. I can do that. Is there anything else I can do for you?" Alba smiles at Yuri's answer and looks excited before she answers:

"I'll get the caviar this time. Sure, I'll tell Liz. A big kiss. Ciao."

Alba reflects for a moment and tells Liz that the interview is over. Liz looks at Alba and says: "Ok. But we should film your comment on the interview here in this room."

She gives Alba a propitious look. Alba nods and whispers:

"Lots of love from Dmitry."

Liz smiles happily and starts to film. Alba ignores the presence of Ahmed who glares at her hatefully. Alba states in front of the camera: "Our world as envisioned by a terrorist and his religion: Holy Wars, Holy Men, commandments and punishments. A contract religion, aiming to make people conform to the wishes of their God. Denial towards everything feminine. Women kept disguised behind a veil, a chador, a burqa. Segregated from any human and women rights, as applied in the free world countries. Women are convicted according to their contract religion of being stoned to death or imprisoned in rooms. Most of these women go insane before they die."

Alba takes a deep breath before she continues:

"Female genital mutilation, also known as female genital cutting and female circumcision, the ritual removal of some or all of the external female genitalia. It is typically carried out by a traditional circumciser using a razor blade or knife in the most cases without anaesthesia. Many of these deeply psychologically and physiologically wounded girls do not survive the torture. Those who do survive, end up suffering for their entire life and are deprived of their femaleness. It is just a barbaric and cruel act, a world without compassion for women".

Alba pauses for a moment. Cynthia's beautiful Buddha statue crosses her mind and she says:

"Furthermore the world is losing its cultural heritage because of acts such as the destruction of the precious Buddha statues at Bamiyan. During former centuries Muslim invaders destroyed the faces and other prominent parts of the statues. Now, though, they have dynamite and destroyed them completely. Their religion banned the worship of idols, showing the human form for the past 1,300 years. Only now, though, do people want to fulfil these demands. However, if we look at the way they treat their women, then the destruction of some statues will not cause them to lose any sleep. A government led by Islamic clerics is an abuse of humanistic values. It's revenge and hate. A world of terror, hate and madness..."

Ahmed starts coughing again, now more violently. Alba isn't able to continue her speech. Nevertheless, Liz continues to film how the two jailers take the prisoner away.

Alba is pensively looking after Ahmed and thinking that this illness caused by hate and terror will rapidly get more and more deadly. With a deep sigh she turns back to the camera continuing with the commentary:

"We have to protect our women, our children, our freedom and democracies. We still have a chance. It is not too late yet."

Liz stops filming and Alba hands the mask to the third jailer saying:

"Thanks a lot. You should have given the criminal the mask."

Part III

Unbroken Bonds

37. I allowed my anger to blind me.

After days and nights of searching the area, Yuri and his men finally find Ali Moussa's hide-out in Georgia, in the Pankisi Gorge, a valley region in the north-eastern corner of the country, bordering on the Chechnyan republic of the Russian Federation.

Yuri feels a surge of anger leading him to seek vengeance the moment he can get his hands on the criminal. He takes his knife and cuts Ali's throat, like the criminal did with many other men and women before. Ali stares at Yuri with deep hatred in his eyes before he collapses and hits his head on a grooved rock slab.

Yuri, caught by his disturbed feelings towards his adversary, is hit by Moussa's bodyguard just a split second before Dmitry eliminates the new threat. Yuri falls on the ground heavily wounded.

Dmitry, Kirill and Sasha approach quickly. They clear blood out of Yuri's mouth and apply a tourniquet around one of his legs as they struggle to save their commander's life.

Yuri perceives loud and strange noises. He is immersed in a yellow light and experiences the feeling that he is sinking into fissures caused by an earthquake. Rock walls collapse around him. Dark clouds drift out of the ground and finally Yuri is sucked into it completely. Dmitry kneels next to Yuri. He opens his eyes looking at Dmitry and says:

"Dmitry, my friend, why did it happen like that? When I killed that bastard I let my anger blind me. In that moment, I forgot about the Lama's words… Only now I remember his words: For the sake of everyone, try to avoid feeling angry. And…", Yuri has difficulty breathing but he continues:

"The Lama also said: Your effectiveness and survival depend on your distance to your feelings. If you don't dissolve even the finest veils of anger or frustration into space, you will not see clearly. Instead, you'll make the same mistakes as your fanatic enemy."

Yuri breathes heavily before he continues: "I'm going to need his help. Go to him."

"I promise, Captain, my friend, I will," Dmitry answers.

Everything starts flickering around Yuri. He cannot hear anything, neither from inside his body nor from outside. He tries to speak, but everything becomes foggy. He hears a very loud noise like a lion roaring. A huge tidal wave rushes towards him with tremendous speed. Engulfed by the power of the wave everything turns white. Yuri's perception of Dmitry and the other men vanish as he is thrown towards a giant fire. It envelops him and everything starts to turn red.

A helicopter is landing. The doctor, helped by Yuri's men, gets Yuri on to a stretcher and they rush him into the helicopter. The doctor then places an oxygen mask over Yuri's face, checks for a pulse and looks for any sign of breathing; both are difficult to find.

Yuri is steamrolled by a noise like a thousand claps of thunder. Flickering lights appear and everything starts to turn green. Yuri is floating between conscious and unconscious states. He reaches for Dmitry. Dmitry takes Yuri's hand and holds it gently. Yuri says with a smile on his face:

"Dmitry, tell Alba I love her. She must keep on working with us. The West needs to wake up and protect its freedom."

Then, all of a sudden everything goes dark for Yuri. He makes three final drawn-out exhalations.

The helicopter goes up. The Caucasian mountains seem to move away beneath it. The doctor becomes frantic and tries to bring Yuri back to life by giving him an injection of adrenaline directly into his heart. Yuri doesn't react at all. Dmitry looks at his friend and Commander. His eyes express deep sadness. For a couple of moments he remains motionless, then he turns around to the doctor and says:

"It's over. Thank you for your work."

The doctor steps back.

The helicopter turns first towards east and the full moon shining there. Simultaneously Yuri hears an echoing Hang. Together with the sound Yuri experiences a perfectly clear, radiant and mild white light like moonlight. He sees his life passing before him, like a movie. Initially the images are very vivid, then they move faster and faster and finally fade away.

The helicopter slowly turns around to the west where the sun is setting. The Caucasus Mountains, immersed into warm ruby red light are left behind. Now Yuri perceives an echoing Ah and experiences a beautiful red light which leaves him in a state of bliss and great joy.

Again the helicopter changes direction. The state of bliss and great joy is first followed by a moment of darkness and then by an intensely bright light. The power of the bright light is too intense for Yuri. He can't stay with it and collapses. There's darkness again. Yuri is dead.

The experience of darkness is followed by a three-day period of unconsciousness.

38. You have great protectors here in Russia.

It is late afternoon in Moscow. Vladimir arranged for Alba and Liz to have their documentary edited in the modern TV studio he is working for. Tolek, the young editor, who speaks English well is in front of the control panel. He saves the edited version of the video and then turns to Alba:

"Are you really sure that you want to have it broadcasted like this? It is very hot stuff. The terrorist won't like it at all. You could put yourself in real danger!"

First, Alba looks at her watch and then at Vladimir:

"We are journalists, aren't we? We have to inform people about what is going on in the world and tell it like it is. We have to be honest and courageous. We journalists shouldn't be cowards like many politicians of today. Politicians consciously lead other people astray or rely on lies, denying our democratic values just to win the next election – they not only confuse others but also themselves and create enormous suffering eventually."

"I agree. Stop frightening the girls! They are only doing their job without any hate or aggression. To inform the world about what is going on is compassion and it helps people avoid actions that create suffering. That is at least my understanding. Alba and Liz are very courageous and brave. Besides, they are very well protected not only because of their motivation but because of their connections as well", Vladimir states.

Alba and Liz smile at Vladimir.

"That's is true. We are well protected. You have great protectors here in Russia", Liz says.

Tolek grins. Liz smiles at him reassuringly and continues:

"You did a very good job. Please, just send it over like it is."

The editor gets up and says: "OK, I'll get you a satellite connection. Your boss, Mrs. Broccoli, will have everything in half an hour."

"Perfect", Alba says, "thank you very much. By the way, do you want to join us this evening at a very special event? A Lama, a Buddhist teacher is giving a lecture about protection of mind."

"Why not? That sounds interesting", Tolek agrees, "which time does it start?"

"At 8:00 pm. The venue is an old- Stalinist-cinema."

"I know the cinema and where it is", Tolek responds.

Alba says with a twinkle in her eyes: "OK, see you there." Alba, Liz and Vladimir leave the TV studio in a very good mood.

39. It will push your viewing figures up.

Alba has booked a two bedroom penthouse suite for Liz and herself, in a little fashionable Boutique Hotel. It occupies a beautiful, 7-storey building and dates back to the 19th century. The hotel's architect has successfully combined luxurious minimalism and an avant-garde style. The hotel is a 3-minute walk from both the Hermitage Garden and Pushkinskaya and Tverskaya metro stations. The penthouse suite is furnished like the rest of the Hotel in a reduced but elegant classical Scandinavian design style.

It is late afternoon. Alba has arranged everything for a candlelight dinner with Yuri on the terrace after the meeting with the Lama. She is nervous. She hasn't been able to reach Yuri yet and he hasn't contacted her. For their date Alba is wearing a short black dress and high heeled sandals; she paces back and forth while speaking on her mobile to Cynthia. From time to time Alba checks the time on her Cartier watch, a gift from her dad when she got her university degree in human sciences. Alba says over the phone:

"Cynthia, of course, the footage we are sending you is not a children's program. Yes, it is insane. It is a world of hate and anger. People need to wake up. Do you want to be forced to hide yourself under a veil, chador a burqa...?"

"Well, if that's the latest fashion", Cynthia jokes.

Alba continues: "Maybe it is not so important to you because you think a veil designed by Vandani is stylish. However, have you ever thought about the fact that such a covering is an advantage for people who want to disguise or conceal their real identity? That might lead to a ban on face coverings in our free countries."

"Aren't you exaggerating a bit here", Cynthia remarks. Alba is disturbed.

"And what about female genital mutilation, also known as female genital cutting and female circumcision? Do you want this to happen to your daughter, Angelina?"

"Stop it! That is enough!" Cynthia orders in a loud voice.

Alba pauses for a moment before she continues:

"If we are weak and refuse to protect our values of freedom and our human and women rights, because we are cowards and prefer to be politically correct, then step by step we help to create a world of tremendous suffering, a world of terror, hate and anger. I will not let myself be part of such a cruel world and scarcity without happiness and joy. As parents, and responsible citizens we need to strive to give our children and all people on this planet the chance of having a good quality of life in freedom. As a journalist it is our responsibility to act now, to speak up and to inform the world about what is going on. If we don't act now what is going to happen soon is our own fault. It is not too late....yet."

"Alba, calm down! I just wanted to test how convincing your arguments are!"

Alba is relieved: "Ok, I understand. That means I can go ahead with A World of Terror and Liz can finish the trailer with the Russian editor?"

Cynthia agrees: "Yes, you can. Go ahead!"

"Thanks. Well, I'm going to see Captain Sokolov this evening to get feedback on his last mission. Actually, he, Liz and I have a meeting with a Lama, a Buddhist teacher...." Cynthia interrupts:

"A Buddhist teacher?"

"Yes, you understood me correctly. We have a meeting with a Buddhist teacher. Among other things I am going to interview him with regard to the subject of protection of mind."

"That sounds like one of your crazy ideas!" Cynthia remarks.

"No, that's definitely not crazy. This interview will push your viewing figures up...", Alba says.

A call is coming in on Alba's mobile. Alba excitedly exclaims: "Cynthia, I have to go. Thank you! I am glad that you support the project! I'll be back in London in time for the presentation. Bye."

Alba takes the phone and feels disappointed for a moment, when she sees that the call is from Tolek, not from Yuri. Tolek inquires kindly: "I hope I am not disturbing you. I am curious about your boss' reaction. Did she like your work?" "I just talked with her. Yes, she liked it and she gave me permission to go on with the trailer." Tolek answers happily: "Wow, that's very good news! Do you think that I could get a job as an editor in your company if the trailer is successful?"

Alba is amused: "Let's see. I think it might be possible." Tolek is satisfied for the time being: "Thanks. See you later."

Alba looks in the mirror and she sees an image she does not want to see. She looks extremely tense. Alba knows this sign very well. It is always the messenger of bad news. Alba sits down in one of the beautiful Danish designed lounge chairs to relax.

Not even two minutes pass until a call comes in on her mobile. It is Liz who is on a sightseeing tour through Moscow with Vladimir on his motorbike. Liz asks Alba if she has heard from Yuri. Alba denies. Liz confesses that she has tried to reach Dmitry several times but his mobile is turned off.

Alba decides to try once more to reach Yuri. Alba presses a button on her mobile phone and holds it at her ear. There's no ringing tone. Alba sights deeply and calls Liz back: "His phone's still switched off. "

"OK, let's go directly to the lecture", Liz suggests. Suddenly, Alba is all smiles: "Liz, there's a call coming in. It must be from Yuri. I'll call you back in a second." Alba happily answers the phone:

"Ciao Yuri!... Oh, it's you, Dmitry! Excuse me. I thought it was Yuri.... No problem. You're on the way, good! Where shall we meet?...Okay. Yes, Toni's with me. See you later."

Alba calls Liz back and says a bit irritated:

"It was Dmitry. He called on Yuri's mobile. Isn't that strange? Anyway, they're on their way. We'll meet them at the lecture."

"That's great! We'll be waiting for you at the entrance",

Liz answers happily.

40. It's like a parachute jump.

Alba arrives late in front of the cinema by taxi. Vladimir approaches Alba and greets her at the entrance. Alba apologizes: "I'm sorry, the taxi was stuck in a traffic jam and I couldn't call neither you nor Liz because I forgot to recharge the battery." Vladimir responds in a relaxed manner: "No problem."

Alba is looking around: "Great. At least she made it. I hope you didn't wait for me outside all that time?"

"Not really. I only checked from time to time if you were here. I got most of the lecture." Alba inquires:

"What about Yuri and Dmitry? Have they arrived?"

"Not yet." Vladimir pauses before he continues:

"Let's go. The first part of the lecture is over. Now it's questions and answers. The Lama responds directly to questions of the audience. It is always very interesting."

Vladimir smiles and gives Alba a ticket. Alba thankfully says: "That is very kind of you. Thanks a lot! How much is it?" "It is a gift and a great joy for me to attend the lecture of my Lama with two beautiful and brave women."

Alba is taken by surprise: "This evening I can't help being astonished. You are a student of this Lama?"

"Actually since 1989 when he first came to St. Petersburg. I was one of his first students." Alba gazes at Vladimir: "Are these people here, all like you?"

Vladimir laughs: "Find out yourself!"

The hall is packed with people. All seats are taken. Therefore, still many stand or sit around the edges of the stage. The Lama sits on the stage with a Russian translator by his side. Alba looks at the Lama. He looks at her. Their eyes meet for a fraction of a moment. It is a moment of recognition and deep understanding. Alba feels deep gratitude and joy arising in her heart.

While the interpreter translates what the Lama just said, the Lama welcomes Vladimir and Alba with a smile and beckons both to a couple of spare seats in the first row. Alba sits down next to Vladimir deeply touched by the Lama and unable to say a word.

The evening is nearly over and people raise their hands for a few final questions. The Lama points to a woman. Sitting next to her is a bearded man and there is some confusion over whom he was pointing to.

"No, no, beauty before virtue", the Lama says jokingly. The woman smiles and asks the Lama:

"Lama, I have some problems at home. My flat is very small and my husband disturbs me. What should I do?" The Lama looks at the woman and asks: "Is it your flat?" The woman nods. The Lama responds:

"First, try with compassion. Difficult people need to be shown more kindness towards them because they are unhappy. The finest compassion goes beyond "like" and "dislike" and can touch even very disturbed people. But if it doesn't work, then kick him out. It's always best to do something on a beyond personal level, something all-pervading and absolute. Here you can work in freedom – it's like a parachute jump."

The Lama looks at his watch and understands that time has come to finish the lecture: "I have to go. I wish it wasn't the case, but we have to finish now. Some important journalists are coming to our centre tonight and it could be really important for our work. I have enjoyed being here again and your questions really show how far we have come. Please visit our centre here in Moscow or wherever you come from in this vast country. We already have over 70 centres in Russia, where my friends and students teach Diamond Way meditations of the kind we just did. When you become one with the Buddha and awareness needs no object, this brings the quickest of results."

While the interpreter translates the Lama's words people get up and head towards the Lama. Immediately he is surrounded by many people. Vladimir touches Alba's arm gently and says: "You should also go to the Lama."

Alba smiles, and tries to weave her way through the crowd. Suddenly Alba finds herself standing in front of the Lama. She is quite excited and her voice trembles a bit when she addresses herself to the Lama:

"Good evening. I'm Alba Smith. We have an appointment." The Lama's blue eyes are deep as an ocean. He looks at her kindly: "Yes, I know. We have an appointment in our centre now."

"Yes, that's right, together with Yuri, the Special Task force officer," Alba responds. The Lama nods. More and more people come close and Alba steps to the side. Without breaking eye-contact with Alba the Lama shouts over the heads of other people: "Alba, do ask at the front door, somebody will drive you to the centre!" Alba smiles and shouts back: "Thanks a lot!"

The Lama turns back to his students and other people standing in front of him for a blessing.

41. In life as in death a hero is a mirror for everybody.

Tolek takes Alba to the Buddhist center with his old car while Vladimir drives Liz on his motorbike.

The Buddhist center is housed in a small 2-story, well restored 19th century building in the centre of Moscow.

When Alba arrives with Tolek at the center on the second floor, the entrance hall, now rebuilt as a modern big open kitchen, is packed with people. They are talking, laughing, eating and drinking. They seem to be very happy to be together. Liz and Vladimir are surrounded by a couple of young Russians, Vladimir's friends.

Vladimir sees Alba first and beckons her and Tolek to join them. He introduces Alba and Tolek to his friends as the journalists who have a meeting with the Lama. Vladimir's friends are very interested in Alba's work, her project about A World of Terror and have many questions for her.

A door opens and Rebecca approaches Vladimir asking: "Where are the journalists?" Vladimir takes Alba and Liz by their hands and introduces them to Rebecca who asks them to follow her.

When Alba realizes that Tolek is staying behind, she turns around and invites him to come along. Tolek smiles at Alba happily and joins the group.

In the Lama's room open suitcases and bags are lying around. The Lama heartily welcomes Alba, Liz and Tolek and invites them to sit with him and Vladimir at the table. Several manuscripts, a mountain of letters and printed e-mails are piled on it.

Rebecca disappears in the adjacent room, where two men are working on their laptops.

A woman brings a bottle of red wine. The Lama opens it and says:

"So this is our Moscow headquarters. Do you like it?"

Alba is looking at the Lama with a radiant smile:

"Well, actually I expected something a little more..."

"Exotic? Celibate? Joyless? This wine's a gift from a good Spanish friend of ours. I'm sure you'll like it."

The Lama pours five glasses and points to the door from where happy voices and laughter are heard.

"We are Diamond Way Buddhists," the Lama says, " we learn to identify the way to highest truth as states of increasing joy. Our meditations make that a certainty. The frame should fit the picture."

Alba is taking out her tape recorder and asks the Lama: "May I tape our conversation and may Liz take some pictures?" The Lama agrees: "Certainly, please go ahead."

Alba gets her tape recorder ready and curiously inquires:

"Please could you explain what you just said? What exactly is the picture?"

"On a practical level, it means living consciously, with a long-term view to benefit others. Being aware that poor countries must stop overpopulation and taking a stand against the suppression of women. It's what you people who work for the media can do best of all", the Lama says.

"Do we?", Alba asks.

"If you are honest and educated, you will do that whether you're aware of it or not. You inform people about terrorism and theocratic states. Many of you surely choose this work for idealistic reasons to actively create a more humane world. I do the same, working with the mental causes, and that's what our fine officers do. Right now, we all act inside the framework of this activity", answers the Lama.

"Well, Captain Yuri Sokolov for example has such dangerous job. His life is always at risk", Alba states.

"At the same time the captain enjoys an access to his inner richness", the Lama responds.

Alba looks at the Lama and asks: "What do you mean?"

"Fighting for something good, while at the same time experiencing love, gives additional meaning to our actions. Acting from anger on the other hand only pulls one into painful illusions."

At this very moment, Dmitry appears at the open door. He looks pale but composed. Liz smiles at him. Dmitry enters the room and respectfully greets first the Lama, then the others. Alba doesn't see Yuri and worriedly asks Dmitry:

"Where's Yuri?"

Dmitry takes a mobile phone out of his pocket and gives it to Alba. Sadly looking at Alba he says:

"I have very bad news. During our last mission the unthinkable happened. Yuri is dead." Alba stares at Dmitry:

"Yuri is dead? Please tell me that's not true!"

Dmitry looks at her and shakes his head. Alba looks at the Lama while tears start to run down her cheeks. Liz is taking Alba's hand and caresses it gently. The Lama is looking at Alba with compassion:

"Remember Yuri by the most amazing things he did. We all die. In life as in death a hero is a mirror for everybody. He truly expresses mind's timeless potential."

He is pausing for a moment before he continues:

"I wish that we had thousands of his kind." The Lama reaches out to Alba and explains:

"According to the Buddhist point of view three days after Yuri´s death his mind will wake up in a state we call Bardo – a transition. His mind then creates a dream world from his strongest feelings, which he will experience as real. As there are no sensory impressions anymore, the subconscious impressions in his mind will begin to surface and he will be drawn ever deeper into its events."

Dmitry nods before he speaks to the Lama:

"Lama, we attacked the place where Moussa was hiding. There was a fight and it was quite intense. At the end Yuri got hold of Moussa and killed him. He cut his throat, just like that bastard did to so many people."

Alba looks at Dmitry startled. Scenes from the cruel footage pop up in Alba´s mind. She starts crying. With sorrow Dmitry takes his eyes away from Alba and continues to tell the Lama what he has promised to his friend: "Yuri was quite angry when killing Moussa. He was asking for your help."

"There's something we need to do. Yuri was a very unusual man. His trust and intelligence have the power to cut through his inner trips. If we focus on those qualities we will reach him", the Lama says.

Alba and Dmitry nod. Dmitry continues his report to the Lama:

"Yuri said also before dying that he would have liked to learn Phowa." He pauses for a moment looking at Alba with a warm smile:

"Yuri said he loves you. He wants you to continue the work you started together."

"Was that Yuri's last wish?" Alba asks. Dmitry nods.

The Lama looks at everybody:

"Yuri`s strength is that he always kept his bonds, in this life and in his former lives. It's my understanding that I was already his teacher then – and you were also there. We used to meditate on this Buddha-form."

The Lama is pointing at a picture, a thangka, of the Kalachakra Buddha form and continues:

"We wanted to secure the world's freedom at the time when our help would be needed. As you know from events around the world we are in the middle of that process now. We all have very important functions to fulfil," the Lama states decisively.

"Yuri is part of our team, he set the stage and we will need him in his next life soon. The world must not lose him to the whirlwind of his personal experiences. If he takes a new human body soon, he can help bring the struggle for our freedom to a successful close in twenty years. Our bond is unbreakable. Everything will be fine." The Lama gets up and the others follow. He indicates that they should not leave yet. He talks with Rebecca in the other room for a moment and comes back with five red strings and five special knots made from blue and red material.

"These are for you. They carry a great energy-field of protection", he smiles, "and it seems that they also work against radar traps on the motorway."

The Lama puts the string around Alba's neck first, then attends to the others. To each string he attaches one of the special knots. He embraces all five and touches their foreheads with his Gau. The Lama asks Alba:

"Yuri was going to come to the Phowa course, which starts tomorrow. I guess you were going to come too?"

Alba nods: "Yes. But now I have to go to St Petersburg for his funeral. I want to be there with everyone."

The Lama thinks this over, then calls Rebecca and asks her where the next Phowa course is. Rebecca steps into the room and says: "We are in England next week, we have a Phowa course there on the South coast."

Alba reflects: "That would be just perfect. I've got to go back to London immediately after the funeral. I need to present my documentary there." The Lama assures Alba:

"Excellent. We will do this together."

42. A magic and powerful moment.

It is the 4th of September 2001 and 3 days have passed since Yuri was killed. Yuri is waking up from the 3 days of unconsciousness.

From this moment on until 49 days after his death at the longest he is going to experience the so-called state of Bardo or transition.

Yuri lies on the ground in front of the cave in the Caucasus Mountains. He is at the hide-out, the place where he killed Ali Moussa and was killed by the terrorist's bodyguard. Yuri starts to move slightly and groans. His eyes flicker and he spits out a mouthful of blood that lands on a black scorpion which has come to investigate. It scurries away. Yuri's vision is blurred. Coloured dots floating in his eyes take the shape of black bearded men who have wrapped camouflage scarves around their heads to conceal their identity. They carry Kalashnikovs and are shouting with rage. One of them has a bazooka, stops and then aims in Yuri's direction. Yuri exclaims:

"Damn! Terrorists!"

Yuri gathers all his strength and rushes forward to the entrance of the cave at the side of the mountain.

The atmosphere is dreary. Strange high noises that are very unpleasant to the ears disturb Yuri while he is picked up by an unexpected gust of wind and pulled in the opening of a tunnel system.

A grenade explodes behind Yuri. He runs as fast as he can to escape the blast. As soon as the smoke vanishes he realizes that there are at least a dozen terrorists chasing him. They come closer and closer. Yuri can already smell them. Just in time he spots a small gap in the boulder next to him. He manages to squeeze through it.

To his great astonishment, he finds himself on a rock shelter in Afghanistan with a breathtaking view on two huge and most beautiful Buddha statues on the other side. Yuri is deeply touched and thankful to be back in one of the most beautiful places he had visited more than 20 years ago.

Back then he was a young Spetsnaz soldier whose unit was based near Bamiyan valley. The Soviet Union had just invaded Afghanistan to replace the existing communist government. Afghanistan's resistance forces, known as the Mujahideen, fought against the Soviet invasion of Afghanistan at that time.

One day, the young Yuri received the order to pick up some food at a farm in the Bamiyan valley. On the way to the farm he discovered the two overwhelming Buddha statues. Standing in front of the two Buddha statues again, he now remembers the magic and powerful moment.

43. You must not get lost in your personal experiences.

Yuri's funeral takes place at the Saint Petersburg cemetery where Sergey's body also found its final resting place. It's a beautiful day. The sun is shining brightly and there is a gentle breeze.

The head Commander of Spetsnaz units stands in front of Yuri's coffin and delivers a touching funeral eulogy. He bestows honour on Yuri by calling him a most brave and loyal soldier of his fatherland, Russia.

In an appropriate distance behind the Spetsnaz Commander stands Dmitry in the place for Yuri's second in command and best friend. Behind him Yuri's unit has formed up followed by Alba, Liz and many relatives and friends. Alba's face shows that she has been crying heavily, but she is trying to hold back the tears now.

After Yuri's Commander has said his formal good-bye to Yuri, Dmitry steps forward and bends towards the coffin. There, he remains quiet for a moment and says to Yuri in a low voice:

"Yuri, my friend, I have seen the Lama. He said that you must not get lost in your personal experiences. He also said that...I think you know what he said... that the two of you have a natural bond."

Alba follows Dmitry and goes right up to the coffin. Yuri is clothed in his dress uniform with all the medals he has received. On his head he wears the Red Beret. Alba places a huge bunch of red roses on the coffin. Then she takes the string with the protector knot she received from the Lama, touches it to his heart and places it in the top pocket of Yuri´s dress uniform. Alba whispers to Yuri:

"This is from the Lama. It's for your protection. The Lama knows the exit, the way out. Your bond with the Lama and many others are unbreakable."

Alba pauses for a moment trying to remember the words of the Lama:

"The Lama and we all wish that you take a new human body soon to help bring the struggle for our freedom to a successful close. Don´t get lost in your personal experiences and do what the Lama tells you! This is an order!"

Alba smiles. With a last loving look at Yuri, Alba whispers:

"I love you".

Then she turns around and walks straight past Yuri, who is standing in front of his own coffin wearing the American Air Force jacket the Lama has given him.

Yuri reaches into the top pocket of the jacket and his fingers find the string Alba has just placed there. He smiles at Alba. Alba does not smile back. Yuri is wondering why Alba is not responding at all to his advances. As soon as Alba disappears from view of the funeral participants she starts to run, rushing to an empty spot behind a tree. Yuri is following her and looks at her worriedly when he sees that Alba is vomiting. When Alba feels better she returns to the ceremony, still with Yuri escorting her.

People are starting to disperse.

44. Killing is not the way out.

Alba is back in London. She arrived from St Petersburg three days ago. Since then she has not left her apartment, not even to contact anybody, apart from Liz.

Alba's apartment in the centre of London is small but rich. The elegant atmosphere is created by a few very valuable pieces from the 17th century, presents of her Florentine grandmother, and warm, intense colours. Some empty mugs and other things are scattered around the room. Alba is curled up on her red sofa in the living room. On the screen of the TV, a scene of her interview with Yuri is still flickering.

Alba is asleep and dreams that she holds the dying Yuri in her arms. All of a sudden Yuri begins to talk sweetly in Russian to her. He reaches up and kisses her. Abruptly he lets Alba go, gets up and turns around.

A masked man with dark eyes stands behind Yuri with a knife in his hand. In a fraction of a second Yuri disarms the masked man, holds the knife to the man's throat and hisses with an ice-cold voice:

"I know you like blood a lot. Now I will show you your own. I'm going to insert this knife slowly into your chest and turn it. Then... I will cut your throat. After about 20 seconds you will lose consciousness and in 2 minutes you will be dead." Shocked, Alba pleads:

"Yuri, no, don't kill him. Killing is not the way out."

Yuri turns around to Alba. The phone rings. Alba wakes up holding her throat. Tears run down her cheeks. Alba presses the bottom of the telephone. The ringing stops.

Yuri sits down beside Alba on the red sofa and reaches for her. Abruptly Alba gets up. Yuri thinks she has pushed him away. She staggers into the bathroom. Yuri follows her. Alba looks at her tear-stained face in the mirror with bewilderment and dismay. Yuri stands behind her. He also looks into the mirror, but there is no reflection of him. Alba looks down at a pregnancy test kit showing two pink lines. The test is positive. As Yuri leans over her shoulder to see what she is looking at, the phone rings again.

Alba walks back to the living room followed by Yuri. This time Alba picks up the phone. It is Cynthia. Alba, trying to remain composed, says:

"No, Cynthia. Of course I would have called you. I just haven't been feeling well since I came back from Russia. I've just been taking it easy for a while. No, no, nothing serious. I'm sorry about the delay. Actually, that's not true, I have some terrible news", Alba says in tears, "Yuri is dead. Sure, okay. I just need to get some things together. I'll see you soon".

Alba goes to the video player to get the tape Cynthia has asked for. Instead of pressing the eject button Alba presses play Ali's face appears on the screen. Alba stares at it for a moment. Yuri turns around to the screen. However, before Yuri can see Ali's face on the screen, Alba switches the video off. She takes the tape out of the video recorder, grabs her bag and runs out of the apartment, slamming the door behind her.

45. He may have been winning for 22 years but now he lost.

Alba arrives at Cynthia`s luxurious residence in Mayfair by taxi. The doorman greets Alba in a friendly way, informs Mrs Broccoli that her guest has arrived and accompanies Alba to the elevator.

At the top floor, Cynthia waits for Alba and hugs her. For a moment the two women remain embraced. Cynthia gently says: "My dear, everything will be fine. Let´s sit on the terrace. Today is a wonderful day."

Alba passes the luxuriously furnished living room. The walls are decorated with a couple of famous original impressionist works of art, and precious sculptures and statues are elegantly placed around the room. Among the sculptures, there is a very beautiful statue of the historical Buddha Shakyamuni. Photos of celebrities as well as her family, her husband Richard and her three daughters, Grace, Ella and the youngest, Angelina, are proudly displayed in guilt-frames on an antique table.

The living room has glass front doors that open on to a big terrace with a breathtaking view over London.

Two dogs, boxers called Max and Moritz lie in the sun on the terrace. They jump up when they see Alba and Cynthia approaching them. Alba smiles and pets the two dogs. Cynthia invites Alba to sit next to her on a big comfortable white sofa while Max and Moritz lay down in front of it. Cynthia remarks:

"Max and Moritz like you. They always feel very comfortable with you."

"Yes, they are very good dogs. They are my friends. I love dogs. I grew up in Tuscany with a Dalmatian called Guapa. She taught me a lot about compassion", Alba responds.

"You mean in your grandmother's Villa, the Duchessa Nerli."

Alba nods. Cynthia's butler appears at the terrace and starts to serve the 5 o'clock tea. For a while Alba and Cynthia just sit on the sofa, enjoy a cup of tea and let the time pass without talking. Then, Cynthia looks at her watch and asks Alba if it is ok for them to watch the video together.

Alba inserts the tape in the recorder located on the terrace. Somehow the interview with Yuri pops up when Alba starts the tape. Alba immediately stops it to rewind it, but Cynthia says:

"If it's not too painful for you, I'd like to watch this as well." Alba sighs and starts the tape. On the screen, Alba sits in front of Yuri in the Hotel room in St Petersburg.

"How would you define Spetsnaz?" Alba asks.

"Win or die." Yuri answers.

Alba continues to ask: "Could one say, that until now, you have always won?" "As you can see, I am alive and in very good health," Yuri responds.

"How long have you been doing this job", is Alba's next question.

"My first mission was in Afghanistan in 1979. That was 22 years ago. Now I am 41."

Cynthia freezes the picture: "Let's start from here. Well, he may have been winning for 22 years but now he lost." Alba is holding back her tears: "Yeah. He lost his life protecting our freedom, protecting us."

Cynthia pours Alba another cup of tea. Alba thanks Cynthia and asks: "Did you like the trailer?"

"Yes, it's well done. Good work."

"The Russian who edited this is looking for a job. Are you hiring, by any chance?"

"Actually, that's very good timing, since Vincent is going to leave us. He ,s getting married to an Australian girl and will move to Sydney. Therefore the Russian editor is welcome. He can start work next month", Cynthia answers.

"That's great. He will be very happy about the good news. Thank you! Are we still going to show the trailer next week as scheduled?"

"Yes, we do! But I have decided to delay the start of the series. Steven is back on A World of Terror and is completing it. He left for Bamiyan in Afghanistan. I liked the new angle you gave the series very much, culture, art...." Cynthia gives the beautiful Buddha statue in her living room an admiring glance, before continuing:

"In particular, your commentary about the destruction of the two Buddha statues enhances the entire project. Steven is getting some in-depth footage concerning this."

Alba is taken by surprise:

"Well, on one hand it is a great joy to hear that you appreciate the new angle I gave the project. On the other hand, I am really surprised that you have sent Steven to Afghanistan instead of giving me the task."

Alba gulps, holding back her tears. Cynthia soothes her with motherly concern:

"It's for your own good. Afghanistan is a dangerous place especially for women. Steven, being a former military and war correspondent is better suited to do this job. I really do think you need some time to get over things. You take A World of Terror too personally. You need to distance yourself. In the meantime, I have something to keep your mind occupied without having to think of A World of Terror and everything involved in it. I need you back in New York, for the The

Rich & Famous series. We need the interview with Harry Rocky and Count Carrano."

"You must be kidding!" Alba exclaims, "certainly I will complete A World of Terror. There's no doubt about that!"

Cynthia does not respond to the issue at hand.

"Do you think it is fair to kick me out of A World of Terror, just now that I gave a new angle to it", Alba continues. Cynthia straight-faced:

"I have scheduled a meeting for you the day after tomorrow at Rossi's headquarters. It's in the World Trade Centre."

"Well, on the 11th I am going to see the Lama here in London to finish the interview we have started in Moscow. The day after that, I will participate in a course given by the Lama, on the South coast. It's about conscious dying. Liz is also coming to film the event. Actually that is necessary to make the new angle successful."

Alba pauses and looks at Cynthia before she continues:

"And a new title for the series is mandatory. The old one A World of Terror does not correspond to the content and the concept any longer."

"And you are telling me all this now in such a reckless tone? Who do you think you are? You are only an employee, a young journalist who has just started her career! Even if your grandmother is the Duchessa Nerli, if you don't want to ruin your career you do what I tell you now!" Cynthia indignantly exclaims. Alba looks right into Cynthia's face and says: "You are right. I am only an employee, a soldier of your company who has to obey the orders of the Commander. Let me tell you that Yuri invited me to participate in the course of conscious dying in Moscow. In the meantime, he died. He did not make it! We can die any moment, you, me, everybody. To be honest, I'm afraid of dying and what might happen afterwards. Aren't you?"

"Hopefully, I will end up in heaven. You know, some kind of a paradise", Cynthia responds.

"Yeah, that's what most people want," Alba looks around:

"But where exactly is this paradise going to be? Your gorgeous apartment with all these beautiful paintings, sculptures and expensive furniture might be paradise for many people. Or do you expect paradise to be something more like a land where milk and honey flow or something like never-ending holidays on a Hedonistic island?"

"Okay, okay Alba. I get your drift. You do look very pale. It might be a good idea to give yourself a break from work for a week or two. Do what you have to do."

Alba gets up: "Ok. Thanks for everything. I will make arrangements for the Russian editor. His name is Tolek." Cynthia gets up as well, touching Alba's arm gently:

"Alba, before you leave I need to know the new title for the series." For a moment Alba scrutinizes Cynthia before she answers:

"It's Where are the Protectors?"

Without waiting for Cynthia's reaction Alba gets the tape and leaves.

46. Swirled around like a leaf in the wind.

Yuri is still hiding in the mountain rock shelter overlooking the Bamiyan valley. He can't take his eyes away from the two large most beautiful Buddha statues.

Out of the blue, Yuri is jolted out of his dreams by cries of great pain and suffering. Yuri jumps into the direction of the mountain from where the cries are coming and finds himself in a tunnel. A strong draught blows into the tunnel. He detects several Kalashnikovs hanging from simple nails in the recesses and cracks along the rock face. Carefully, not wanting to get torn away by the strong draught, he squeezes his body against the rock face to get hold of one of the Kalashnikovs. Just as he manages to grab one, he loses his balance, is blown away and swirled around in the tunnel like a leaf in the wind. He has no control over his body anymore. Finally he is hurled against a boulder in a cave.

Everything goes black.

47. Those qualities are the hooks to catch him and set him free.

It is early morning of September 11, 2001. Alba enters the terminal of Heathrow airport and heads towards the arrival gate. A crowd of people is waiting. Alba approaches a young man who looks like he is waiting for the Lama: "Are you waiting for the Lama?"

He confirms and asks Alba if she has come for the Phowa course. Alba nods and asks:

"Is it your first Phowa?"

"Yes, it is. I am quite excited", he responds with a big smile.

The Lama has arrived at the arrival gate followed by Rebecca and a group of his students who are travelling with him around the world. He receives a warm welcome from his friends and students. The Lama hugs each of them, exchanges a couple of words and laughs. One can tell that he is happy to see them all.

Alba stands back from the crowd. The Lama looks up, notices her and walks over. He kindly says:

"Alba, come with me." The Lama takes Alba by the hand and heads towards the exit.

A car is waiting to bring him and his friends to the London Buddhist center. Anthony, one of the Lama's old students, is at the wheel. The Lama sits next to Alba. He puts his arm around her shoulders. Tears well up in Alba's eyes:

"I gave Yuri the blessing string and the protector knot you gave me. I thought it would be good for him wherever he is now. I've had some very intense dreams and he always seems to be close by. Does Yuri know he is dead?"

"Only for short glimpses, if at all. There is too much going on and he hasn't really meditated before. This is where his connection to me and his attraction to you will become useful. Really, do try to remember everything great and beyond-personal Yuri did. Those qualities are the hooks to catch him and set him free", the Lama explains.

Alba looks directly into the Lama's face:

"What do you mean?"

"Our whole existence is like a dream on several levels. From a good dream one can wake up into liberation and enlightenment. Disturbing actions however bind you and create more difficulties and suffering. This view unites mind's relative and absolute levels", the Lama responds. Alba smiles at the Lama: "Do you think you can help Yuri find a good dream to wake up from?"

"We will do this together. You know it's all about idealism, courage and lasting friendships. And talking of dreams, I had this most interesting one this morning," the Lama pauses for a moment before he continues,

"actually Yuri should have some idea about this. After all it was his job. Let me share it with you all."

Rebecca, Anthony and another young man stop talking to each other to hear what the Lama has to say.

48. The Dream.

The dream takes place in a cave in the mountains of Afghanistan: The Lama is sitting at a table opposite a tall man who has a dark beard and wears a white turban. Behind the man with the turban, there is a TV on.

The Lama is looking at the man:

"Tell me something. Is it true, that you or any man who has created vast spiritual merits by killing infidels cannot go to your paradise if they are sown into a bag made from pigskin?"

Smoke starts to come out of the man sitting opposite him and his body shrinks. The Lama continues:

"And what about the fact that you cannot live in a street if certain Arabic words are written on the wall? Is it true, that you simply have to purify constantly?"

Just as he said this, Arabic writing appears on the wall and as a result the man with the dark beard and white turban dissolves into dust.

49. Without attachment, everything in life becomes a gift.

The London Buddhist center is located in a town house, a 3 story building in the center of London.

The Lama and his students have arrived and are now sitting at a large table having lunch. A business woman in her late 40s has just finished asking the Lama a question. The Lama jokingly answers:

"So that's your question, can we invest in our next life? Do you mean deposit money in a bank? Well, I don't think we have institutions that would accept a concept like that? Our money-men just believe in one life! Better to invest in the here and now. Try to be useful in every moment and enjoy the karmic interest later. Through giving to others you will know your own richness and they will be generous in the future. Cause and effect always function. Actually, the best way to become timelessly rich is to dissolve one's expectations. Without attachment, everything in life becomes a gift."

Alba looks at Liz and remarks: "Cynthia would have asked something just like that." The business woman continues to ask:

"What do you mean by attachment?"

"Holding on tightly to something that you think will make you happy. In the long run, it will only make you more dependent. No outer object can experience happiness. Only your mind can experience it, so that is where you should look for it. The only meaningful thing to take into your next life is a stock of good impressions in your mind, your enjoyment of freedom and the wish to help others...", the Lama pauses before he continues: "and some good friends and a teacher or two to remind you of where you once got to."

The business woman wants to ask more questions. The Lama turns towards the door. A beautiful Scandinavian-looking woman stands at the door and says with a shocked expression:

"Something unbelievable has just happened. An aeroplane crashed into one of the twin towers at the World Trade Center!"

Alba is appalled: "My mom works there and that is where I should have been myself doing an interview right now...." Everyone scrambles towards the stairs and to a room with a TV on the top floor.

The Lama and his friends and students arrive upstairs and see another plane just crashing into the south-tower of the World Trade Center. The Lama remarks, looking at the screen:

"Terrorists!" He turns to Rebecca and says:

"We've got to get in touch with everyone we know in New York."

Everybody gets busy. Rebecca gets her Palm out and starts reading out telephone numbers while different friends use their mobile phones and start making calls. Alba is also on her mobile and sighs with relief when she finds out that her mom is alive due to the fact that the office was moved to Soho a month ago. Nevertheless, she is a little irritated that her mom did not inform her about the moving; she experienced of moment of great fear that she had died in the terrorist attack.

Liz is next to Alba. She tries to reach Dmitry a number of times, but to no avail. Finally she gives up and helps Rebecca call the Lama's friends and students in New York.

Alba, still talking to her mom on the mobile, raises her head for a moment and meets the Lama's eyes. He smiles kindly at Alba and nods. Alba hears herself saying to her mom:

"Stay where you are. You're safe in Soho. I'll take the next plane I can catch and come over. Yes, we'll follow everything on TV. Liz is just calling a friend to get some more information. I'll call you back, okay? I love you."

50. I'm the perfect weapon!

Yuri wakes up from his collision with the boulder. He immediately spots heavily-armed and black-masked men who guard a large modern electric security gate, the exit and the entrance into the cave.

One of them catches Yuri's attention. On his right hand one of his fingers is missing. Yuri stares at the man until a grinding and very unpleasant noise coming from the opening of the security gate irritates him and becomes the target of his attention.

Up the slope, three military jeeps drive into the cave. Just after the last jeep has entered, the gate is closed in a hurry.

However, before the gate completely closes a black dog with beautiful amber-coloured eyes sneaks in and runs past Yuri. The armed men jump out of their vehicles and rush into one of the tunnels.

Not missing a beat, Yuri follows them until they stop in front of a bolted and barred rusty iron door. The leader of the masked men takes out his mobile and bellows two words into it. After quite a while the rusty iron door opens. The masked men step through it, hold up their Kalashnikovs and shout:

"God is great!"

Yuri steps a little closer and spots a long-bearded man with a white turban who is sitting in front of a TV. Although more than 20 years have passed, Yuri immediately recognises the terrorist-leader Mustafa ben Ammar. During the Afghan war, Yuri, who was a very young Spetsnaz soldier then, had the honour of catching the criminal who was later exchanged for General Chevalkov and General Korsakov. Looking at the terrorist-leader, Moussa's picture pops up in Yuri's mind and he says to himself:

"Where ben Ammar is, the toad, his favourite and most "talented pupil", can't be far away."

A Kalashnikov rests on the criminal's lap. He's surrounded by more than a dozen bodyguards whose eyes are glued to the TV screen.

Ammar announces euphorically: "Now we have proof! Our operation against the great Satan of our world was successful. This is the grace of God. He has given us much happiness."

Yuri doesn't hesitate. He aims at Ammar and pulls the trigger. His gunshot is followed by a siren. One of the bodyguards pushes the man with the white turban to the ground. They open fire and shoot wildly towards Yuri. Several bullets hit him, but nothing happens. Yuri shoots back. The bullets of his Kalashnikov hit five of the bodyguards but they don't show any reaction.

The terrorist with the missing finger hastily approaches and drags the black dog with the amber-coloured eyes behind him heavily massacred. The saggy dog's head is bleeding. The terrorist hysterically shouts:

"It was this beast! He sneaked in and set off the alarms!" Fuming with anger, he takes his knife and cuts the dog's throat.

Yuri runs a few steps and then jumps. He flies through the air towards Ammar. A bullet from Ammar's Kalashnikov passes through Yuri's body harmlessly and hits the forehead of the man who killed the dog.

The dog killer sinks to the ground landing on top of the dead animal.

Yuri kicks Ammar's throat. Ammar collapses and starts to shake. One bodyguard shouts:

"Quick! Get his medication! The general is having one of his attacks!" A second bodyguard nervously takes a couple of pills out of a bottle, throws them into Ammar's mouth and pours a glass of water after them. Yuri looks at Ammar amazedly:

"I did my job well. I killed him. He must be dead."

Yuri touches his body where he was hit by the bullets. His hands go straight through his body unable to catch hold of anything. Again he grabs at his body but his hand simply passes through. For a moment Yuri is surprised, then his face lights up as he realizes and says to himself:

"I don't have a body anymore. Nothing can harm me anymore. I'm no longer a target."

He pauses before he shouts with relief:

"I'm the perfect weapon!"

Yuri roars with laughter. The roar gets louder and louder and is transformed into the noise of a giant turning wheel. Yuri is sucked into its centre by its energy and loses contact with everything.

51. The world will have to come to grips with the real cause of its instability.

Although the Lama and his students are glued to the TV where the crashes are shown again and again, all eyes are immediately on Rebecca when she enters the room. With a radiant smile on her face she announces:

"We have just finished contacting all our friends in New York. They're all fine. Not one of them was anywhere near the towers. Frank was the closest and the luckiest. He works at the south tower but was late. His wife had just switched the TV on, just as he was leaving the apartment, and saw the first plane crash into the north tower."

Everybody is relieved. They hug each other in support and gratitude. Liz again is trying to get through to Dmitry but again without success.

Alba approaches the Lama in front of the TV and asks:

"Lama, would it be possible for you to say something now in front of the camera? Something about how we can avoid more killing and suffering in the future." The Lama nods and says:

"Certainly. I think it's important to take a position on what is happening here and now."

Liz positions the lights and attaches a microphone to the Lama's shirt. Alba takes a little mirror out of her bag. She puts on some lipstick and brushes her hair. The Lama smiles at Alba: "Beautiful woman." Alba thanks the Lama with a radiant smile.

Liz signals that she is ready to start. The Lama sits on the couch; as customary in interviews, Alba is in front of him. Liz directs the camera to Alba's face. Alba says into the camera: "What just happened today, on the 11th of September, looked like a scene of a horror film. Unfortunately, it wasn't just a film – we can't just look at it and then switch it off whenever we wish. Today many people died. They were killed in an act of terror."

Alba pauses for a moment, looks at the Lama and continues:

"With me today is a Lama and Buddhist teacher, who plays a leading role in the survival of Diamond Way Buddhism after the destruction of Tibet." Alba turns to the Lama and asks:

"Lama, how can we avoid more killing and suffering in the future after today's tragedy?"

"Our Western democracies should prepare our excellent mental institutions for those responsible rather than think first of killing them. They would clearly qualify as clinically paranoid and the public awareness of their disease would not inspire many future martyrs. Very soon, however, the world will have to come to grips with the real cause of its instability: the uneven fertility of different populations. The ultimate aggression occurs when minorities out-breed other cultures or groups. Around the equator, most countries today are poor due to overpopulation. It will therefore be exceedingly wise to collectively pay people to keep their families small. If we are quick and use all the means at our disposal, future tragedies can be avoided. If we do not act, then we are just at the beginning of what will become unending suffering", the Lama answers.

Rebecca steps in, pointing at her watch. She is dressed in motorbike leathers. The Lama looks at her and asks:

"Is it time to leave already?" Rebecca nods.

The Lama addresses Alba and Liz:

"Thank you. We have to leave now. Let's continue later on. Now, we're going to the South coast for the Phowa course. I am really looking forward to the motorcycle ride. I have 143 horsepower on two wheels and many curves. Wish us luck that there are no police on the way! Are you coming?" "Yes, we are coming! I am riding a Kawasaki Ninja ZX-6R", Liz excitedly replies.

The Lama smiles: "You certainly are an excellent and focused motorcycle rider."

Alba confirms: "She is indeed." Liz smiles happily.

52. Yamaland.

The giant wheel Yuri has been sucked into, slows down and Yuri jumps back to his feet. Behind the wheel is Yama, the Tibetan Lord of Death. This time he looks like a warrior. He is heavily armed and wears shiny armour. With one strong tug of his colossal claw-like hands he stops the wheel and looks at Yuri:

"Warrior, welcome to Yamaland. This is just a little taste of what's yet to come. To get out of here, you need to be more than just a perfect weapon."

Yama roars with laughter and disappears in the wheel which again turns so fast that Yuri faints.

When Yuri comes back to consciousness he is surrounded by heavily-armed and black-masked men. In a split second, Yuri jumps to one of them and puts his knife to his throat. The black-masked man says with a pacifying voice:

"We are not your enemies. We are your escorts to help you fulfil your mission."

"What mission?", inquires Yuri. The black-masked man responds:

"The mission to find Sergey's murderer." Yuri is still not convinced:

"And who is the murderer?" The black-masked man answers without being disturbed by Yuri's aggression:

"It's Ali Moussa." He pauses for a moment before he continues:

"We know where he is hiding. We'll bring you there."

"Tell me where he is!" Yuri orders in a commanding tone.

The black-masked man answers:

"He is trapped in a world of hate and terror."

Yuri lets the black masked man go and says:

"Well, it is not my intention to rescue him. To hell with him."

Yuri checks his watch and addresses the masked-man who hands him a Kalashnikov:

"How much time do we need to get to his hide-out?"

"It depends on you. The only thing I can say about time, is that you have 39 days left to fulfil the mission."

"Then let's move!"

The 12-men escort take Yuri into their midst. Yuri is about to object that there is no need for protection, since he is a protector himself. Instead he just gives in. Yuri holds the rifle at the ready position and runs along the murky light labyrinth with his protectors. A variety of strange and awkward noises echo through the tunnel. Yuri's protectors run at high speed through the murky lightened tunnel. Yuri is forced to focus on his protectors to keep pace with them.

Finally after a race that seems to last for days the murky light is getting brighter and changes into gentle soft lights of different colours which lead into a battle arena, an Amphitheatre. Yuri is overwhelmed by the magnitude of the colossal Amphitheatre which is at least 108.000 times bigger as the Flavian Amphitheatre, the Colosseum in Rome he had visited during a secret security conference more than 10 years ago.

The arena is packed with countless beings of all shapes, sizes, colours and appearances. Some of them look like they have escaped from Disneyland. Yuri's protectors push their way through the crush of beings whose eyes are captured by pictures on an oversized 360° screen showing an impressive teaser campaign about the six different worlds of Yama and their protagonists.

The entrances to each of Yama's six worlds are either tiny hatches or big gates guarded and controlled by beings disguised like the protagonists of Yama's trailer.

Each hatch or gate is bathed in a soft light in different colours; there's soft white, soft red, soft green, soft yellow, soft blue, and smoky grey.

Crowds of beings are lined up in front of the tiny hatches and big gates and are eagerly waiting to enter the worlds they're attracted to.

Yuri orders his 12-men escort to stop. He is intrigued by a trailer about a world bathed in soft white light:

A splendid palace appears on a divine hill. For Yuri it looks like Petershof, the palace of Peter I outside of St Petersburg. It seems to be in its most glorious days of the Russian empire, and it dominates the entire scene. On the large staircase decorated with colourful statues of Greek gods and fountains, men and women of unforgettable beauty and elegance walk towards the entrance. Thousands of candles create a sensual inviting light. A banquette is taking place in the palace. The beauties who are dressed in luxurious garments dine at a table made from the finest Italian marble. Handsome waiters and waitresses serve exquisite dishes in crystal, silver and golden vessels.

In the park, water streams out of the countless fountains. Its luminescence turns the mild light into countless rainbows. As soon as they dissolve they change into a fine golden rain descending on the divine beings sauntering in the park. With great elegance, they jump into the fountains filled with champagne. There are exotic fish shining with all colours and lofty swans. Dances take place on a golden platform to the accompaniment of heavenly music. At some distance the most beautiful wild cats are watching the scene...

Yuri gets distracted by a man with oily black hair dressed in an expensive but gregarious suit. He rushes towards an extraordinary good-looking man who seems to be taken by what is going on the screen. On his way, he bumps into a fat and stupid looking guy of uncertain origin who is munching on a hamburger, drinking beer and holding some porno magazines. The man with oily black hair hisses to the stupid looking man: "Piss off!"

To Yuri, who is interestedly observing the scene it seems that the fat man wants to say something but instead he drops his magazine, hamburger and beer-can and staggers away with his mouth open wide. Disgusted, the man with the oily black hair approaches the extraordinary good-looking man, and points to the fat man:

"What a pig!" The good-looking man does not respond. He is immersed and fascinated by the trailer playing on the screen. The man with oily black hair touches the man's arm and says in a tone just trifle too friendly:

"Sir, where do you come from?"

The good-looking man turns around irritated and says proudly:

"From Hollywood."

"Oh, really! You are a film star?"

The good-looking man is highly delighted to be recognised as a film star and answers:

"Yes. Do you remember me?" The man with oily black hair lies:

"Of course I do. How could anyone forget somebody like you? Actually I'd like to give you a little gift. Something very special and very precious. It's really the best quality available." The film star smiles showing his perfect teeth:

"Well, I love gifts. What is it?"

The man with the oily black hair takes out a little envelope and hands it to the film star saying:

"The stuff that dreams are made of."

The film star's face takes on a hard impression when he states:

"I don't want such a gift. It makes you look old and ugly. I can't afford to be old or ugly."Annoyed, he turns away from the man with the oily black hair.

Two long-legged divine beauties which could have played a part in the trailer, approach the film star, take him into their midst and walk away with their heads held high.

Yuri looks for a moment after the two long-legged divine beauties before he turns to the man with the oily black hair and demands:

"Let me see the goods."

The man with oily black hair is only now taking notice of Yuri and answers in a disparaging tone:

"I don't think you could afford this stuff. I know you don't have a lot of money. But maybe we can do business. You're a man with important connections."

Yuri commands his escort: "Arrest him!"

53. The Greedy One.

The man with the black oily hair takes flight from Yuri and the 12-men escort. A scary and disgusting-looking creature gets in his way and stops him. It is grey-skinned, has a tiny wrinkled head, and a mouth no larger than the eye of a needle, in contrast to its enormous belly. In a scarcely audible voice it asks the man with the black oily hair for something to eat.

The man with the oily black hair is actually repelled but as he feels Yuri following him he quickly throws the package with the white powder towards the creature who grabs it greedily and hurries away towards the hatch illuminated by a pale yellow light.

However, the man with the oily black hair is not happy at all about giving up the white powder that belongs to him. So he chases the creature and gets hold of it just before it jumps into the yellow-lit hatch which is guarded by two other creatures that look exactly like the grey-skinned one.

The man with the oily black hair jumps on the creature and thrusts his fist into the creature's face to make him let him go of his package with the powder. Although the creature is beaten up brutally by the man with the oily black hair, he doesn't let go of the goods.

Finally the creature is helped by the two guards who kick the man with oily black hair savagely all over his body. He cries out in pain. The only way out for him in order to escape his torturer, Yuri and the 12-men escort is to jump into the yellow-lit hatch. And that is what he does.

As soon as the man with the oily black hair has disappeared behind the yellow-lit hatch Yuri shakes his head in disbelief and mutters:

"What a fool!"

Yuri turns around to his escort to inform them that the fool has trapped himself by jumping into the yellow-lit hatch but to his surprise there is no 12-men escort anymore. Yuri disapprovingly mutters to himself:

"Damn. I must have lost them while hunting the greedy one. The heck with it. The only thing that counts is to fulfil my mission."

54. With high speed towards freedom.

Southern England near Brighton. A line of motorbikes travels on the curvy roads of the Sussex coast that forms a wide, shallow bay between the headlands of Selsey Bill and Beachy Head. A red traffic light stops the motorcyclists. The Lama, with Rebecca riding on the back on the motorbike, leads the line. As soon as the traffic light turns green he speeds up, closely followed by Liz and Alba on the Kawasaki Ninja ZX-6R and a good dozen of other motorbikes. The Lama's sparkling blue eyes behind the visor express great joy to ride 143 horsepower on two wheels and to share this experience with his students on the way on the way to his Phowa course.

55. Problems only have the power that we give them.

After the first agitation about having lost his escort, Yuri is back to reality which for him, means back to fulfil his mission to find Sergey´s murderer. He pushes harder through the crowd to recover the lost track of his protectors. Nevertheless, it seems like they have fallen off the face of earth.

An excited crowd, absorbed by what is going on the oversized screen bathed in soft red light, bars Yuri´s way. The screen catches his attention. It depicts a gigantic huge tennis court. Aristocratically looking men and women sit on the grandstand and follow the match. An athletic beautiful-looking young and confident woman stands in line to enter a huge gate bathed in gentle red light. She turns to Yuri who is next to her, amusedly watching the tennis match. The confident young woman says to Yuri:

"I'm going to win my seventh gold medal today. What about you? You look like someone who's never lost a battle!" She hands Yuri a racket from a large collection she is carrying and tells him to follow her.

A middle-aged woman, who looks Russian and is wearing a head-scarf turns to Yuri sadly:

"Oh, what did I live for? I worked all my life, and then I lost all my savings during Perestroika, and my only son, whom I managed to give an excellent education he became a member of a gang." Yuri answers her in Russian:

"Well, that's life. We try to get what we like, avoid what we don't like and adapt ourselves to the things we cannot change. Problems only have the power that we give them."

The Russian woman is walking away muttering to herself:

"What is he talking about?" Yuri ironically remarks to himself:

"Well, I am very good at giving advice to others...."

Yuri turns around to catch up with the young confident woman.

Looking around to keep track of her, his eyes get caught on a scene played on the screen which is bathed in a soft yellow light: It shows a kind of post-apocalyptic rubbish dump with scenes a' la Breughel and Bosch. The dump is overpopulated with countless pale-skinned beings with tiny mouths, enormous bellies and exhausted faces. They are crawling around on the rubbish desperately looking for something to eat. The only thing that they can find is garbage and eventually a few crumbs of rotten bread which immediately become the cause for a fierce fight in which adversaries are cut to pieces.

The one who is fortunate enough to get a hold of a bread crumb immediately puts the captured good into his tiny mouth and swallows it. In the next moment a heart-rending cry startles Yuri and the creature is suddenly writhing about on the ground in great pain.

The man with the black oily hair appears on the scene. He remains indifferent to the great suffering of the creatures around him. He is euphoric and cannot stop laughing at the stupid creatures. He triumphantly holds up the package with the white powder. The creatures run up to him and beg for the powder. He asks the begging creatures what they can give him in return. They respond that if he has compassion for them he will find the way out of the rubbish dump. He responds sarcastically:

"Is that all you have to offer? Compassion is not of interest to me. What can I buy with compassion?"

The creatures fall on their knees in front of him, begging for mercy. As he continues to refuse, his mouth becomes smaller and smaller. He starts to panic, takes some of the powder out of the package and tries to eat it. To his horror that's very difficult because his mouth has become very small. Finally he manages to swallow some of the white powder.

Nevertheless, his greed is only satisfied when he has finished the whole package. Looking at the hungry creatures around him with great satisfaction, he dumps the empty package on the dirty ground. The hungry creatures tear into the package.

Only one moment later the man with the oily black hair squirms on the ground in unbearable pain. His belly is growing bigger and bigger. Finally, he looks just like one of the creatures he is surrounded by.

Yuri sighs and turns away from the scene.

56. There's nothing I can rely on here.

Yuri scans his surroundings for his 12-men escort once more, and this time he gets distracted by a white stretch-limousine which pulls up in front of him.

The doors open. In the back of the car there are the two long-legged beauties who had picked up the extraordinary looking man before. They invite Yuri to enter. Yuri bends down toward the gorgeous ladies with a charming smile. He smells a divine fragrance. One of the blond beauties whispers into Yuri's ear and awakens his senses:

"We are in charge of picking you up and bringing you to a banquet held in your honour. All of the most important dignitaries are present to honour your deeds and merits as a soldier."

Yuri is about to enter the limousine when his eyes catch a scene on the huge screen reflected in the outer mirror of the limousine: It depicts the extraordinary good-looking man whose appearance is changing rapidly. He's getting older and older. The despaired expression on his face leaves no doubt that he is distressed by the knowledge that he, too, is going to die. His divine companions are aware of what is going to happen. They no longer stay at his side but blow kisses at him from a distance, send their good wishes and eventually abandon him.

Utterly alone, the dying good-looking man is engulfed by sorrow and stumbles down huge stairs towards a red-lit gate. Even though he tries to stop his flight down in front of the red-lit gate, he continues to fall as the stairs become steeper and steeper. With enormous effort and with all his strength he manages to stop in front of a soft blue light which lights a big gate.

Before running into the gate he takes a fast look downwards. His eyes are caught by a soft-green light and wild animals such as jaguars, cheetahs and tigers. For a moment he is taken by the beauty of the animals but then he runs into the blue-lit gate. An older and plump woman with a warm and inviting smile on her face embraces him.

Yuri shakes his head in disbelief, straightens up and says to the two beauties:

"I'm sorry, but I can't stay with you. There's nothing I can rely on here. It's better if I go back to work. I still have a mission to fulfil."

57. Warrior, hurry up! The battle is starting soon!

Yuri still indulges in the divine fragrance of the two blond beauties when somebody grabs his hand and drags him away. It is the confident young woman. She shouts: "Warrior, hurry up! The battle is starting soon!"

Yuri has difficulty freeing his hand from the iron grip of the woman and stumbles behind her. In front of the gate bathed in a soft red light, the confident woman slips on a banana skin. She lets go of Yuri, floats straight ahead through the gate and disappears.

A moment later, Yuri recognises the confident young woman on the screen. She watches healthy looking women and men gifted with gorgeous, athletic bodies in competition with each other and is eagerly waiting for her turn to compete.

From time to time the competition is interrupted by scenes of people tearing shopping bags from each other's hands, fighting for seats in restaurants, for places in queues at bus-stops and in banks; these scenes are fading in and out again.

The winner of the tennis match, a strong and athletic looking blond man is announced. The young confident woman approaches and challenges him to fight a tennis match. As their tennis match becomes more and more ferocious the scene changes into violent demonstrations which take place in the streets and eventually take over entire countries. Soldiers fight bitter wars in the night. It becomes increasingly difficult to tell friend from foe in the darkness. Helicopters circling high in the heavens prepare to drop their deadly load. The fighting escalates. Now warriors equipped with heavy military attire and holding guns, walk into an enormous battlefield.

Yuri gets excited. He wants to enter the gate bathed in red light. Instead, a sudden gust of wind swirls him around and he detects his 12-men escort on the other side of the battle arena.

58. A young couple tenderly make love.

Yuri keeps sight of his protectors while pushing through the crowd.

To his dismay he's again trapped in the midst upon thousands gathered in front of a screen lit by soft blue light, fascinated by what is going on: A young couple tenderly make love. The blue light becomes more intense as does their lovemaking. The Russian woman Yuri met before stands close to him. She looks at the scene in excitement and addresses herself to him smiling sadly:

"That's what I was always looking for in life. True love."

After these words she and many others run towards the open entrance illuminated by blue light to join the couple who are making love.

The screen above Yuri's head is now showing a happy Russian lady making love to a young well-built man drawing Yuri's attention. Many other people are doing the same.

Slowly, the love-making scene fades out and a new one comes up showing how one baby after another is born and how the number of people multiplies rapidly. The dark-skinned babies born in poor countries without freedom are more numerous while the fair-skinned babies born in free countries are fewer.

In the meantime, Yuri notices very few people sitting in deep meditation somewhere up.

As the blue light starts to fade the crowd vanishes until there is nobody left in front of the blue-lit gate.

59. Confusion and Ignorance.

Yuri, finally without being blocked, departs and rushes in the direction where he spotted his protectors before. As he runs off he bumps into the fat man who falls on the ground. Yuri apologises and helps the fat man to get on his feet. It appears to Yuri that the fat man's head has changed somehow. It looks like a pigs' head now. Even so, his body is still the same.

Yuri realizes that the whole environment is bathed in a soft green light and he hears noises of two boars which are mating. The noises are coming from the teaser shown on the screen. The fat man is as excited by what is going on the screen, as are many others of his kind. Everybody pushes to be the first to enter a hatch illuminated by green light. There is much confusion.

The fat man is one of the first to enter the green-lit hatch followed eagerly by many others. As soon as the fat man and the others have disappeared behind the hatch, the screen shows the fat man with the pig's head running behind a bush where the noises of the mating of the boars are coming from. A moment later he is coming back into view transformed into a real pig.

Scenes of animals being hunted, misused and eaten by other animals or killed and tortured by humans follow. The animals are continually amassing harmful impressions in endless rounds of killing and being killed. The only happiness animals seem to experience is to bring up their offspring and take care of them.

That is what pops up in Yuri's mind as he looks at the screen and sees a cat happily watching her five beautiful playful kittens playing with each other. Yuri turns away from the screen with sorrow.

On the ground empty beer cans, half-eaten hamburgers, porno magazines and other junk the fat man and his kind have left behind lie carelessly discarded. Yuri sighs:

"What confusion, what ignorance. I am wondering what is happening with people who are politically correct. Maybe they transform into chickens and end up in one of these chicken farms..."

An objectionable whiff of foul-smelling odour and desperate cries for help set Yuri off. He starts running.

60. There is no joy in being right when one is foretelling disasters.

The line of motorbikes and cars reach the final location of the course, a campsite in the countryside. As they slowly pass a big tent, the Lama enthusiastically remarks to Rebecca who is in the back of the motorbike:

"Great, this time there will be enough space for everybody."

The line stops in front of a little wooden house where a group of people eagerly await the arrival of the Lama.

He and Rebecca get off the motorbike and hug and greet them warmly. On the way to the little house the Lama takes his and Rebecca's luggage. Immediately two strong young men offer their help. The Lama says to the two strong guys:

"Thank you. I get food every day, so I should also work a bit. This is the only sport I have the chance to do. Do you have a TV?"

The group enter the little house. In the middle of a spacious room is a big table set up with food, but nobody seems to be hungry or interested in it.

The Lama and everybody else in the room are concentrating on the news on TV: At 13:04 American time US-President George W. Bush states that the terrorists who are responsible for this act will be hunted down and punished.

Immediately a discussion starts what should be done now. Everybody wants to know what the Lama thinks.

"First, let's write an e-mail to all our centers around the world," he responds. Rebecca sits down beside the Lama and opens her lap-top on the table. All the others gather around the Lama while he composes an e-mail:

Dear friends, there is no joy in being right when one is foretelling disasters. As has been increasingly evident for decades to those who dared look, theocratic extremists have placed themselves on a track where they can only go from bad to worse. It is now up to our permissive western democracies to accept the challenge and protect our women and institutions in effective ways.

The Lama pauses for a moment before he continues:

I ask you, my students in the US. and all around the world to use a period between 68 and 72 hours after the blasts to do many Om Ami Dewa Hrih – Mantras. Please meditate on the Buddha of Limitless Light above southern Manhattan where the collapsed skyscrapers stood and above the Pentagon further south along the American East Coast. We should not do Phowa and transfer their minds into a Pure Land as hardly any of those who died will be Buddhists. Invoking the essence of compassion, however, will benefit beings in ways they can understand. All our love from the English countryside, Yours Lama".

The Lama gets up, excuses himself and leaves the room.

61. Damn! Am I trapped?

The battle arena is nearly empty now. Although nobody blocks Yuri's way, he can hardly see because of the steamy, foul-smelling air which gets denser and eventually transforms into murky smoke.

Yuri can only trust in his ears and follows the desperate cries for help which are coming closer and he understands that the bastard he is looking for is not far away. This insight stimulates him to hurry up and eventually he is stopped by his 12-men escort in front of a hatch bathed in smoky grey light.

Yuri gets his Kalashnikov ready and orders his 12-men escort to follow him into the hatch to charge the citadel of the bastard and rescue his victims. The men don't move. Yuri shouts: "That is an order!"

The escort's leader stands in front of Yuri and says in a firm tone: "Commander, you can't go in there. It is a trap with no way out."

Through the smoke, on the grey-lit screen, Yuri makes out a post-nuclear wasteland with a few black ruins and carbonised tree stumps. The air is filled with smoke and flames. The scene looks unbearably hot. Whining and moaning sounds are interrupted by inhuman screams. Silhouettes of several enormous vats can be seen, polluting the air with boiling-hot steam. Crippled creatures wander about or cower fearfully on the ground. Steep ladders lead up to the top of the vats. Men with masked faces and black gloves grab the whining creatures and drag them up the ladders. The creatures beg for mercy.

The men with masked faces laugh hysterically while throwing them forcibly into the vats. Glowing lava splashes out in all directions. Yuri, horrified by what is going on the screen, is nevertheless ready to fight for his entrance when he realizes that his escort is gone. He brings his Kalashnikov at the ready and storms in the direction of the hatch bathed in smoky grey light.

One pace away from entering the hatch, he is attacked by the black dog with the beautiful amber-coloured eyes who was killed before. After a short fight the dog surrenders. Yuri orders him to stay outside and guard the gate until he returns. The black dog only seems to obey Yuri's orders.

As soon Yuri has entered the hatch, the dog sneaks in and sticks to Yuri's heels. Yuri rushes towards the victims. The black dog stays behind him. As Yuri gets closer, right before his eyes, the whole scene changes dramatically.

All those who were once tortured exchange places with the torturers and their cyclical relationship begins again. Yuri stares at the scene in disbelief and says to himself:

"What's going on here? That's madness!"

Shaking his head he turns around and heads toward the exit, the hatch he has entered through. It has vanished. There is no way out, only smoke, flames, boiling vats and screaming creatures as far as his eyes reach. Yuri is upset:

"Damn! Am I trapped? I have to get out of here! I have to find the exit."

62. The promise to protect the freedom of people everywhere.

The Lama sits down in the bedroom of the little wooden house and meditates. His mind moves through time and places and stops in Tibet in the 1930's. He and Yuri are busy fighting Chinese troops. With others the Lama, Yuri and Alba make a promise to protect the freedom of people everywhere. At first Yuri is distracted and kills a passing fly. Then he focuses.

Yuri, trapped in a world of hate and paranoia closes his eyes for a moment. He sighs, touches his heart and feels something in his breast pocket. He pulls the object out of the black leather jacket the Lama gave him. It's the red string with the protector knot which Alba had put there. He smiles and wraps it around his neck.

As he moves his head he feels that somebody is staring at him. Yuri looks upwards and sees Ali standing high up on a ladder guarded by his bodyguards, smiling maliciously. He holds a creature with its face over the boiling water. Ali is shouting down at Yuri:

"Come get him!"

Yuri points his Kalashnikov up at Ali and shouts back:
"I will get you!"
With a resolute gesture Yuri throws away his Kalashnikov and slowly climbs up the ladder.
Ali is laughing hysterically while Yuri comes closer and closer.

63. Water purifies.

Rebecca silently enters the room. The Lama still sits in meditation position. Rebecca gently touches his arm and says: "It's already eight o'clock, you should go to the tent. Everyone is waiting for you".

The Lama nods, remaining for a few more moments in meditation position. Then he gets up embraces and kisses the young woman saying:

"Not lazy times these, are they?"

Rebecca smiles at him and nods. Tenderly he lets Rebecca go and disappears in the bathroom.

The Lama turns on the tap of the washbasin. At first nothing happens, then some water spurts out. The Lama concentrates on Yuri saying:

"Yuri, water purifies. Do you remember the Buddha Diamond Mind? We used to meditate on him together. Right now he is setting you free."

64. People must be quite sick to do these kinds of things.

Yuri climbs higher up the ladder. Ali stops laughing. He rolls his eyes and his movements become more and more distorted while he still holds the screaming creature. Yuri focuses on Ali and calmly says:

"Poor guy, you must be really unhappy if you want to do things like these. People must be quite sick to do these kind of things. This is hell."

Ali shouts at Yuri: "No one is going to get out of here alive! Especially not you, Comrade!"

Ali takes a couple of grenades and throws them at the vats. Then he gives the screaming creature a push. It plunges, but Yuri rescues it.

One water-filled vat explodes, flooding everything. Screaming beings are drowned by the mass of water.

Ali and his bodyguards enjoy the suffering of the creatures from their position high up on the ladder.

65. Use every event to free yourself.

The Lama walks to the big meditation tent with Alba and Liz. Liz tries once more to reach Dmitry on his mobile. This time he answers. Liz happily chirps into her phone: "I have finally reached you, darling! Are you okay? Great! I am with the Lama. Ok, I'm passing him the phone." Liz informs the Lama: "Dmitry would like to talk to you." The Lama says into the mobile:

"Dmitry, I've had contact with Yuri several times during meditation. Please think of all the great things he's done. That will make his way easier. Now, I will pass the phone back to Liz."

The party reaches the meditation tent. Liz remains outside to continue her conversation with Dmitry while the Lama and Alba enter the tent.

Inside, it's packed with people who stand in little groups and animatedly talk amongst themselves with a lot of smiles and laughter.

The Lama gets up on the stage and sits down on a seat with a meditation cushion. A young man approaches to clip a microphone to the Lama's shirt.

Alba finds a place for her and Liz to sit in the first row next to the young man she met at the airport. The young man is absorbed in a conversation with a young and pretty woman who looks Russian. Alba sits down on the floor and is mesmerized by a thangka behind the Lama, above his head. It depicts the Red Buddha and is extraordinarily beautiful. She is deeply touched by the Red Buddha's beauty and remains enchanted until Liz stands in front of her and says:

"Dmitry confirmed the destroying of the buildings today were terrorist attacks carried out by some of Yuri's old rivals. Everything should be okay now and you should not worry about your mom's safety anymore." Liz pauses before she continues:

"He also said that he is on constant alert and therefore not allowed to leave Russia. He can't call me but I can still call him. Of course, he's very upset about the situation. At the end of our conversation he said that he will come to England to visit us as soon as he can."

Alba smiles at Liz: "That's very good news! Thanks a lot."

Liz takes a seat on a meditation cushion on the floor beside Alba who whispers to Liz that the two good-looking men behind them have been so kind to give their meditation cushions to them. Liz turns around and thanks the two young men with a great smile.

On the stage the Lama makes a "hrrr" noise. The talking stops. The younger people sit down on the floor on meditation cushions and the older ones on chairs. The Lama lets his eyes wander over his students and announces:

"I am very happy to see you all and thank you very much for coming. Some of my students...", he winks at several men and women before he continues:

"...made the big effort to travel here from far away. I thank you very much. It is such a big joy for me to see you all." The Lama pauses a moment before he says:

"As you know something terrible is unfolding in America right now and so I've decided to change the program. We will go straight into singing one round of the Phowa text you have been given. Everybody, please join in. If you are new to Phowa you should see the singing as an introduction to the meditation, which you will learn directly after-wards. I want all of you to think of people you know who died between three days and 7 weeks ago and I shall include them in the power-field. I am going to be calling in and transferring the mind of the bravest man I know. He belongs to the power-field of the Buddha of Limitless Light."

The Lama shows a stack of letters and pictures to his students:

"Last year the sailors in the Kursk submarine were very prominent in our minds when we did Phowa. Now it is the brave soldiers who are protecting the freedom of our women around the world. There will be time for questions later. This is where we start the meditation."

Alba, Liz and everyone else start to concentrate and sing the Phowa-text. After a while Alba's mind wanders to the beautiful thangka of the Red Buddha of Limitless Light, also called Amitabha. She feels an unmeasurable joy arising in her heart. It seems to her that the Red Buddha above the Lama's head transforms into crystal-clear red light and radiates with the brilliance of a mountain of rubies on which the setting sun shines.

The Lama concentrates on Yuri:

"Yuri! You were always intelligent. Your mind is wherever you think it is. Now follow me to the Pure Lands. Really use every event to free yourself."

66. We will all get out of here.

In the cave another vat explodes. More water flows in all directions. The level of the water increases and the cries of the creatures for help are getting even more desperate. To escape drowning in the boiling water they try to climb up the ladders. Immediately, they are attacked by Ali and his henchmen who still enjoy the scenes of endless suffering below them. A cloud of foul-smelling steam covers everything.

The boiling water has nearly reached Yuri now, and it's still rising. Yuri carries the creature he has rescued on his back. He has noticed that the creature's right hand is missing a finger. He climbs further up the ladder faster than the water rises and focuses on reaching Ali and his henchmen.

The Lama runs out of the tent and rushes towards the bathrooms while the participants of the course sing on. While he's washing his hands the waters stops flowing again. The Lama bends down, looks under the sink and then hits one of the pipes with his fist. After a few gurgling noises, more water flows from the tap. With an impish grin, the Lama quickly finishes washing his hands and face.

In the cave, the remaining vats explode. Huge amounts of water flood the cave. Yuri has climbed to the level occupied by Ali and his henchmen. As Yuri comes closer Ali laughs hysterically at him, opens the jacket of his uniform and shows him the dynamite that is packed around his body. He shouts:

"You are going to stay here and die suffering like all the others. Listen to how they scream", proudly he continues,

"I am a Mujahideen who has fought a Holy War against the unbelievers. I will be a martyr and I will be rewarded in paradise. We are promised that if we fight for the cause of our God, whether we slay or are slain ourselves, we will return to the garden of paradise. There he will wed us to celestial virgins, pure and beautiful, and unite us with large-eyed beautiful ones while we recline on our thrones set in lines."

Yuri shouts back: "Suicide is not the way out for anyone. You will only suffer even more. You will die again, again and again. To stop killing is the only way out of this hell, and a world of unending suffering."

Yuri looks at the suffering beings around him and continues talking to Ali in a very loud voice that everybody can hear:

"I will promise you something. We will all get out of here. My mission is to free beings."

At lightning speed, Yuri takes the knife he killed Ali with in the Caucasus and carves something in the ceiling of the cave in Arabic letters. Above him a crystal red light appears. The light is very strong but Yuri is able to focus on it. He concentrates on it while finishing his writing.

The Lama's still in the bathroom. With joy and a sense of release he pulls the washbasin's plug. The collected water flows out, spinning in a circle.

The Lama runs back to the tent, sits down on the stage and continues the meditation practice. His students sit in deep concentration. They now send their minds to the Pure Land of Buddha Amitabha. A serene smile appears on the Lama's face.

Yuri finishes writing the last word – and at this very moment, the world of unending suffering is gone. Now, there is only brilliant red light.

67. Whoever promises to protect others will always do well.

Yuri sits in front of the Lama in meditation posture with closed eyes. Beside him sits the black dog with the beautiful amber-coloured eyes. Yuri opens his eyes. The Lama smiles at him. Yuri jumps to his feet. The black dog does the same. Yuri puts his hands on his heart and bows his head towards the Lama slightly.

The Lama takes Yuri by his neck and presses his forehead against his own. Yuri says with tears in his eyes:

"Lama, thank you! Now I am free!"

While the Lama holds Yuri in this position he smiles and says to the black dog:

"In your next life, my friend, you will be two-legged!"

Alba opens her eyes. They are full of tears but she smiles happily at the Lama. The Lama nods joyfully.

The meditation session is over. Everybody gets up. Immediately the tent is filled by the vibrant noise of happily talking students.

The Lama makes the "hrrr" noise again. The talking stops immediately and everybody pays attention to the Lama's words:

"We have a lot to celebrate but also a lot to learn. When we have understood the nature of mind we should take rebirth for the benefit of others again and again. Let us celebrate the idealism and power we all share! Whoever promises to protect others will always do well. I will see you all tomorrow morning for the next round. Good night."

The Lama jumps from the stage.

Epilogue

Due to the 9/11 tragedy, Cynthia cancels A World of Terror indefinitely. Alba is asked to work on the series The Rich & Famous but declines the offer and is therefore dismissed. For Alba, this decision turns out to be a chance to travel with the Lama who is about to leave Europe to give his yearly teaching-tour throughout the United States.

In New York, at a public lecture, Alba introduces Lucrezia, her mother, to the Lama. They seem to have a natural bond. On the same evening Vladimir arrives from Moscow to join the Lama's teaching tour as well.

While travelling with the Lama Alba and Vladimir develop an original idea for a book, a thriller. The story is about freedom and liberation, inspired by Yuri's life as a hostage-rescuer and an anti-terrorism expert.

The Lama is very enthusiastic about the idea and comes up with the book title for the thriller: The Second Coming of John Smith. At first Alba is surprised about it. As she continues to write the story at her grandmother's villa, and collaborates via e-mail with Vladimir, she begins to understand more and more that this title is just perfect.

The Duchessa witnesses with great joy not only the birth of her great-grandchild Dianora, Olga, who is named after her and Yuri's mother, but also the completion of Alba's and Vladimir's thriller. She is moved by the story and has tears in her eyes when she finishes reading the book.

She tells Alba that now she can die happily. Before dying, however, the Duchessa strengthens her bonds with Alba, her daughter Lucrezia and Vladimir and makes wishes to meet them all again in her next life to help secure the world's freedom.

Not long after that the Duchessa dies in the presence of Alba, her daughter Lucrezia and Vladimir with a sweet smile on her face.

One year later Alba and Vladimir marry in the Tuscan villa which now belongs to Alba. Many friends from near and far attend the wedding. Liz and Dmitry, Alba's and Vladimir's best man and witness arrive a couple of days before the wedding with their 6 months old twins, John and Gregor. As Alba looks at the two identical twins in the the baby carriage, Gregor is the first one to wake and stare up at her with his beautiful and alert amber-coloured eyes. Alba smiles at him and whispers:

"Who are you with such lively, gorgeous eyes?"

Just then, John wakes up and familiar brilliant blue eyes are beaming at her. Happily she takes John's little hand and says in a low voice:

"You did not get lost! You made it, you are back!"

But still she wonders who Gregor is; he has such unusual eyes,....

In that moment the neighbour's dog passes by and barks...

The Second Coming of John Smith becomes a bestseller and eventually Hollywood buys the rights to make a movie out of it. Alba and Vladimir win an Oscar for the best screenplay.

About the book

*"All that is needed for freedom is to cut through
mental expectations and habits.
Mind then frees itself and all is a gift."*
Lama Ole Nydahl

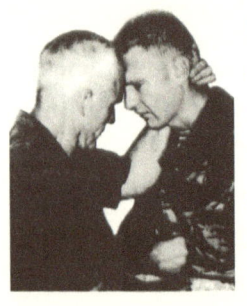 Exit Here is a novel, a fiction, about love and free-
dom and the courage of those who protect it. The
story takes us into an unknown and breathtaking
world in which it becomes evident how the power
of wishes for the benefit of others and bonds remain
active from life to life.

These strong bonds and wishes come alive between
Captain Yuri Sokolov, a Russian hostage rescue and anti-terrorism expert,
Alba Smith, a courageous young Italo-American journalist Yuri falls in
love with and a western Lama, who is a Buddhist teacher and an expert
on death, intermediary state (Bardo), and rebirth.

Yuri Sokolov meets the Lama shortly after his youngest man was killed
by his worst enemy, the terrorist Ali Moussa. Yuri finds himself telling the

Lama about the death of his teammate. To his surprise, the Lama not only promises him to take care of the fallen soldier, but also tells Yuri about a Tibetan Buddhist method called Phowa taught by the Lama himself in order to enter a state of highest bliss at death, a method able to change peoples lives. Yuri is eager to learn this method and decides to participate in a Phowa course the Lama is holding in Moscow.

Before the two men part the Lama tells Yuri that his effectiveness and survival depend on his distance to his feelings. If he does not dissolve even the finest veils of anger or frustration into space, he will not see clearly. Instead, he will make the same mistakes as his fanatic enemy. The longer he is under fire, the easier this can happen.

He urges Yuri to be very careful and for the sake of everyone, to try to avoid feeling angry.

Not much later, the unthinkable happens. Yuri dies during his mission hunting down Ali Moussa.

Yuri's second in command informs the Lama about Yuri's death. He tells the Lama that Yuri let his anger blind him and, already fatally wounded himself, he killed Moussa in a moment of feeling anger. While dying Yuri remembered the Lama's words and asked for his help.

The Lama immediately acts by inviting everybody to remember Yuri by the most amazing things he did and says that in life as in death a hero is a mirror for everybody.

For Yuri, the adventures are far from over. He now enters a world beyond the known one and his experiences feel as real as they can be.

He encounters Yama, the Tibetan Lord of Death and many strange beings in bizarre situations while only just becoming aware of his own death.

In the end, Yuri has to confront Ali Moussa once again and gets trapped in a world of hate and terror.

It doesn't seem like he is going to escape... to find the exit...

A note about the author

Bea Franz was born in Germany. She got her degree in Rome, Italy, in "History of Art and Costume Design". Exit Here is her first work to be published.